Flans and Felonies

Pelican Cove Cozy Mystery Book 16

Leena Clover

First Published – March 30, 2025

Contents

Chapter 1

The island town of Pelican Cove was experiencing a cold winter morning. It was the middle of January and the wind sweeping the beach was harsh enough to blister skin and make eyes water.

Jenny King stood on the porch of the Boardwalk Café, gazing at the horizon, sipping a cup of coffee. The Atlantic Ocean spanned her line of vision, its waves rushing up the sand and retreating in a rhythm of their own.

The town was finally seeing a lull in the tourists after the holiday season. Many business owners breathed a sigh of relief, glad for some respite before spring arrived. Jenny's café had a steady business from the locals but it was nothing compared to the dozens that thronged her café in summer and fall. She was thinking about following the advice she had received at the latest meeting of the Main Street Shop Owners and go in for a bit of renovation. She thought a fresh look would cheer everyone up but was not prepared for the pushback she would receive from her own set of friends.

Betty Sue Morse had shot down the idea at once.

"Absolutely not, Jenny." She set her knitting down and glared. "Are you determined to erase whatever little we have left of Petunia?"

"What are you saying?" Jenny deflated. "I will always be grateful to her for leaving me this café. Not a day goes by when I don't think of her."

Molly, the quietest of them, nodded vigorously.

"We all miss her, Betty Sue. The Magnolias are incomplete without her."

Star launched into an old story about their friend. Petunia, the original owner of the café, had been a fixture in town until her sudden demise a few years ago. They had been surprised to discover that she had bequeathed the café to Jenny King.

Heather Morse set her phone down and plunged into the conversation.

"You're stuck in the past, Grandma. Jenny has to think about turning a profit. Look at that chair you're sitting on. Scuffed from decades of use. It could use a bit of polish."

"I have nothing against a fresh coat of paint and new polish." Betty Sue put Jenny on the spot. "But that's not all you're thinking of, are you?"

With a sigh, Jenny agreed her friend was right. She was thinking of hiring an interior decorator.

"The kitchen sink is cracked. No amount of scrubbing can rescue that ancient subway tile backsplash. And the roof in the dining room leaks."

Betty Sue offered to give her the name of the local handyman.

"I have a meeting with Shirley Brown this afternoon," Jenny confessed. "She did a fine job at the Steakhouse. Jason and I both love how she made the place look more contemporary."

"Brought it into the twenty first century, you mean." Heather laughed.

Betty Sue stuck her lower lip out and commenced knitting at a frantic pace. Jenny glanced at her aunt Star, feeling wretched. Maybe she should drop the whole idea.

"We can look at the designs when they are ready," she cajoled. "I won't approve anything until we all agree on it."

Betty Sue gave a grudging nod and asked for coffee. They spent the rest of the morning discussing the New Year Eve's party Jenny and Jason had hosted at Seaview. Her son Nick and her ex-husband Billy had been conspicuous by their absence.

"When do they get back?" Molly asked, darting a sly look in Heather's direction.

"How should I know?" she growled.

Jenny rubbed one of the tiny gold charms that hung around her neck on a chain, thinking about Nick. He was back from his trip to Mexico and Billy was bunking with him, reluctant to come back to his home in Pelican Cove.

"Isn't it time you made up?" Jenny bristled. "You have to stop acting like a child, Heather. The poor man put his heart on a plate and handed it to you."

"And she tromped on it!" Betty Sue boomed. "I don't care if you remain single all your life, girl. But don't you grow into a surly and bitter old woman. Have a heart."

Star pointed out a seagull cresting the waves, desperately trying to create a diversion. Billy had delivered a romantic proposal in the fall, sure about the outcome. Heather had shocked them all by turning him down.

The Magnolias had tried to tackle her several times since then but she had been tight lipped on the subject. None of them could figure out the reason for her decision.

"You led the poor man on," Betty Sue accused. "He worships the ground you walk on and this is how you pay him back? For shame!"

Heather just left the room whenever they mentioned Billy. Jenny thought it didn't bode well for their group. He would always be a part of her life since they had a son together. Plus Billy was now a fixture in Pelican Cove. He had easily won over the locals with his ready laugh and generous disposition.

"I have to go." Molly stood up and gathered her books. "See you later at the town meeting."

The group broke up, going their separate ways. Heather didn't linger as she usually did. A wall had gone up between them since the doomed proposal. Jenny had tried to gain her young friend's confidence several times but hadn't made any progress.

Star stuck around and opted to make a pot of soup. Jenny made a small batch of chicken salad sandwiches for her regular customers. Many expected them for lunch regardless of the season.

They finished washing up and prepping for the next day after their own meal. Star yawned and glanced at the clock in the kitchen.

"Why don't you go on home?" Jenny offered. "I can meet this woman on my own."

"Are you sure you don't need some company?"

"I'll be fine." Jenny smiled. "The woman's a decorator, not a seasoned killer."

"Don't even joke about it," Star pleaded.

Jenny sat on the deck, stirring sugar in her coffee, enjoying the quiet around her. The tide was in and she was soon lost in admiring the dance of the waves as they battered the beach, a vista that always calmed her.

A woman came down the boardwalk, wrapped in a red wool coat, wearing high heeled shoes that elevated her petite frame.

Jenny wondered if this was the decorator. They had spoken on the phone but never met in person.

"Hello!" she waved a greeting as she came closer. "Am I late?"

Jenny stood up to greet her.

"Welcome to the Boardwalk Café, Shirley."

She was a short woman with generous curves who needed the four inch heels to come up to Jenny's height. The jersey dress she wore was figure hugging and in the latest fashion, not the kind you got in your regular departmental store.

"You're gorgeous!" Jenny was spontaneous. "And those highlights were not done anywhere on the Eastern Shore, I bet."

Shirley threw back her head and laughed, agreeing Jenny was right.

"Isn't that blasphemous? A native islander would never disparage our town like that."

Jenny assured her she did not mean any insult. She was just being honest. And she wanted the number of the person who could work that kind of magic with hair color.

"Oh, don't worry about ruffling my feathers." Shirley waved a hand around. "I'm an outsider, just like you. Although I've been here a lot longer than you have."

Betty Sue had not mentioned knowing the woman and she was aware of every little thing that happened in Pelican Cove. Shirley must keep a low profile. It was hard to believe that as

Jenny took in the bold woman sitting before her. She was just shy of brash.

Jenny offered coffee. Shirley accepted readily, asking for something to nibble on.

"I need to eat every hour or my blood sugar plummets." She illustrated it by raising her hand and swooping it down like an airplane. "Do you have whole milk?"

After Jenny fixed the coffee to her guest's liking and assured her she only used real butter in her cookies and not margarine, Shirley finally relaxed.

"You must give me a tour of this dump." She sprang up after she drank half the coffee and nibbled on a chocolate chip cookie. "I see I'm going to have my work cut out for me."

Jenny ignored the rude comment, assuming it was a ploy to get more money.

"Nothing drastic," she hastened to explain. "I just need a fresh look. And I can't keep the café closed for long."

Shirley didn't answer, heading inside straight to the kitchen. She spotted all the flaws and pointed them out.

"I need two weeks just for the kitchen. You must get rid of this ancient range. We can put up a stack of ovens right here, all stainless steel."

Having two ovens was a dream. It would be a big help if Jenny could have one oven for her muffins and pies and another for roasts and casseroles.

"You think there's enough space?"

"Sure!" Shirley was confident. "We'll knock down these built-ins. They belong in the seventies."

The budget was brought up and Jenny told her time was her main constraint.

"There's one more thing ... this café is my friend Petunia's legacy. I see her presence in every corner and I must preserve that. This cannot be another commercial café."

Shirley whirled around and patted Jenny's arm.

"You're sentimental. And that's fine. The client's needs are paramount in any job I undertake. Don't you worry about anything."

They toured the main café area where Shirley pointed out the wobbly chairs. Jenny grudgingly admitted a lot of customers had complained about them.

Jenny asked about the timeline. Shirley needed two or three days to come up with the designs. She could start work as soon as Jenny approved them.

"There might be some corrections."

"Unlikely!" Shirley dismissed. "I get things right the first time."

Jenny explained how the Magnolias would also have to approve what they did.

Shirley began shaking her head, her brow settling in a frown.

"Are they going to dilly dally over the paint samples? I don't think this is going to work, Jenny."

They were back in the kitchen, Jenny examining the place with new eyes. Did the cabinets look shabbier than usual?

"You must be used to dealing with different members in a family?" she quizzed.

"Yes, yes." Shirley clucked. "But I have a time crunch. We need to be done by the end of the month, at the very latest."

That worked for Jenny since February was the time when couples visited the shore to celebrate Valentine's Day.

"So do I. Sooner the better. Do you have another project lined up?"

For the first time since she had arrived, Shirley was evasive. She proposed putting in a window above the sink. It would provide a view of the beach and bring in some natural light.

"I have shortlisted a few other designers." Jenny thought it was time to be firm. "It's okay if this is not up your alley."

Shirley pursed her lips, admitting the project had sparked her interest.

"I would love to bring this quaint café to life, Jenny. But here's the rub. I may be leaving Pelican Cove for good."

Jenny tried to curb her curiosity. She didn't know Shirley well enough to question her decisions. But the woman didn't have any qualms about sharing details of her personal life.

"Let's say, things are not that great right now. I could use a change."

Chapter 2

The sun had already set when Jenny started for the town hall with Jason and Star. Twilight lingered near the horizon and the sky was painted with ribbons of orange and pink. A chilly wind blew, ensuring the party had all bundled up in their warmest coats.

"What's the purpose of today's meeting?" Jason asked. "I hope it's something more interesting than the case files I was working on."

"There's bound to be some fireworks," Star chuckled. "When have we ever had a town hall meeting that was not full of conflict?"

They laughed and threw around ideas about possible topics they might encounter that evening. At least most people had taken down their Christmas lights. Jenny reminded them about the bitter quarrel that had sprung up in the last meeting among two neighbors. Each claimed the other had too many lights and ornaments in their garden, disturbing the peace of the neighborhood.

Betty Sue was calling the meeting to order when they trooped in and walked to their usual places in the second row. Molly waved and motioned them to hurry up. Heather was nowhere to be seen but a familiar figure sat beside Molly. Billy was back.

"Hurry up and sit down, Jenny." Betty Sue rebuked over the microphone. "You're holding us up."

Suitably chastened, Jenny sat down with a thud, trying hard to suppress a giggle. Betty Sue pounded the gavel and brought up the first item on the agenda, the winter festival.

"Not this again," Jason mumbled under his breath.

Jenny knew it was a recurring topic. Some people were lobbying for a winter festival to drum up business in the otherwise slack months of January and February. Others thought it was too much effort since they would hold the spring festival later that year.

"Why are we talking about this?" Ada Newbury, the richest woman in town, complained imperiously. "I thought we laid this silly topic to rest last year."

There were some murmurs in the crowd and the arguments began. Molly's neck swiveled from side to side as she traced the voices. But she was too meek to ridicule them. Jenny missed Heather's comments, acerbic but laced with wit.

"How are you, Jenny?" Billy leaned toward her. "All good?"

She threw the question back at him.

"Does this mean you are over her?"

Billy's face crumpled.

"I shouldn't have gone away. Nick thinks I acted like a coward."

Nothing can be more painful than losing your child's respect. Jenny decided to call their son the moment she got home and give him a piece of her mind. What had he said to Billy?

"He was supposed to cheer you up."

Billy squared his shoulders. "I'm not giving up. Even if I spend the rest of my life convincing Heather ..."

The noise around them had risen to a crescendo. Two or three camps were formed and the usual arguments were presented. Tempers flared and insults were hurled across the groups. Betty Sue pounded her gavel again and again, unable to control them. Finally, the sheriff blew on a whistle and warned them to settle down.

"I will close this meeting right now if y'all can't be civil to each other."

Jason bumped a fist in the air and hailed him.

"Go Adam!"

He received a silent warning in response and Adam asked him to zip his mouth.

Jenny began to stand up, assuming they were done. But there was another item on the agenda. Betty Sue peered at a paper she held in her hand.

13

"Phyllis Tross wants to file a complaint. Are you here, Phyllis?"

She rove her eyes across the room. A woman in the back stood up. Jenny saw a dense, snow white bob but could barely see her face.

"Why don't you come forward, hon?" Betty Sue smiled.

Star leaned closer and whispered in Jenny's ear. The woman belonged to Betty Sue's knitting club.

A pert woman wearing a navy blue dress and a matching sweater came forward. She wore a strand of large pearls around her neck and pale pink lipstick. Her brows were plucked thin and arched like small hillocks.

She walked to the podium in a steady gait and stood at an angle, glaring at the crowd. Betty Sue cleared her throat, nudging her to move on.

"I am being targeted. Never thought I would live to see this day, Betty Sue. Pelican Cove has become unsafe for older women on their own. Why, I might be murdered in my sleep."

Adam Campbell came forward, his mouth set in a grim expression.

"Hold on, Mrs. Tross! Do you mean someone harmed you? Why haven't you informed the police?"

She gave a snort and brushed him off.

"This is not a job for the police. This scoundrel needs to be driven out of here. Only the town committee can help me with that."

Betty Sue urged her to elaborate. Phyllis breathed fire at some obscure point in the crowd and began. Jenny guessed the object of her wrath was present in the room.

"I'm a retired toll booth operator and a widow. All I want is to live my sunset years in peace, tending to my garden. But that's too much to ask, apparently."

She had a penchant for growing flowers and was very successful. The thorn in her side didn't come from her rose bushes. Her neighbor plucked the flowers in her garden as soon as they bloomed, leaving it bare.

"That's him, right there. Paddy Benson. A sorry excuse for a man!"

Her quarry chose to ignore her and remained silent, managing to irk her more.

"Don't just sit there, pretending you're innocent. Own up to your crimes."

Betty Sue prompted him to come forward.

A lanky six footer wearing faded jeans and a sweatshirt stood up and waved.

"Hello everyone. I have no idea what she means. Phyllis, mate, are you taking your medicine?"

Laughter rang out and Jenny saw the woman turn red. She felt sorry for her. The man she was accusing seemed to be in his sixties, a lot younger than Phyllis. And he had a strange accent.

"What proof do you have, huh?" he needled. "Have you actually seen me do this dastardly deed?"

"You shameless cur! I can see them in that hideous vase you place in your living room window, and beside your bed."

Paddy asked why she was spying on him.

"You're a peeping Tom, aren't you, Phyll? The Sheriff might have something to say about this." He placed his hands on his hips, growing serious.

Adam had to step in. "Are you pressing charges?"

"No Sir! I just want to point out this little lady should watch her words. She's a pain in my neck, you know."

Phyllis began to splutter and her eyes assumed a stricken look. Betty Sue came to her rescue.

"Don't try to muddy the waters, Paddy. This is a serious allegation. Stealing your neighbor's flowers is strictly against the law here. A precedent was established in 1987 when the town committee levied a five thousand dollar fine for the crime. I won't hesitate to make a similar ruling."

Paddy gave her a mock bow.

"I get a flower delivery from the city twice a week. The best orchids, tulips, birds of paradise ... nothing as ordinary as primroses."

With a sigh, Betty Sue informed her friend they needed solid evidence before taking any disciplinary action. The meeting finally broke up.

Jenny grabbed Jason's hand and tugged.

"Let's get out of here."

A voice hailed her and came closer, removing any chance of escape.

"Hello Jenny!" Shirley Brown walked up with the man Paddy in tow. "Let me introduce you to my partner. This is Patrick Benson but everyone calls him Paddy. He's the most easy going guy you'll ever meet."

Paddy placed an arm around her shoulders and pulled her close. He gave Jenny a wink.

"I'm Australian. It comes with the territory."

"That's why your accent sounded familiar. We met an Aussie guy on a cruise we took a while back. You sound a bit like him."

He flashed a sheepish grin and brought up the Boardwalk Café.

"Shirley here told me what a bonzer place you got. I've been there a few times. Your chicken sandwich is a ripper."

Jenny was impressed by Paddy's knowledge on various topics. He had been raised on a sheep station in the Australian Outback and obviously came from money. He had a lot of ideas about how the Boardwalk Café could be bigger and better. Jenny couldn't help being drawn in.

"Franchising is the ticket. That's when you'll begin to rake in the moolah. Shirley here can help you create a brand kit. A nice logo, huh? Point me to your accountant. I can work with him to create some attractive projections. Then we approach investors."

"No, no." Jenny tittered. "You're way ahead of me. I told Shirley the café is my friend's legacy. She was not interested in expansion."

Paddy stepped closer, giving her a wink.

"Who's going to know? Surely your mate wouldn't grudge you a bit of money? Nice nest egg to retire on."

Where was Jason when she needed him? Jenny looked around for her husband but he was nowhere in sight. Star had come to stand behind her.

"He's gone to Mama Rosa's before it gets too crowded."

Getting pizza after the town meeting was a tradition they all cherished. Jenny said goodbye to Shirley and Paddy and promised to think about his suggestions.

"I'll have the designs in a day or two," Shirley nodded.

The couple left and Jenny waited a few minutes to give them a head start.

"What a gasbag!" Star muttered. "We better head home soon. The others are already there."

Jason stood outside the pizzeria, almost hidden behind a stack of large boxes. He placed them in the back seat next to Star and got in. The car filled with the savory aroma of tomato sauce and herbs. Jenny's mouth watered.

"This is torture. Seems like ages since we got Mama Rosa's pizza."

Billy paced the driveway when they reached Seaview.

"She's not here."

Jenny propelled him inside, reminding him he needed to be patient.

"You should stop going after that foolish granddaughter of mine, Billy." Betty Sue patted his arm when he swooped down to kiss her cheek. "She doesn't deserve you."

Molly began handing out plates and Jenny didn't waste any time biting into a hot slice. Nobody spoke until they had taken a few bites.

"Do you believe your friend?" Molly asked Betty Sue.

Dissecting what had happened at the meeting was as much of a ritual as the pizza.

"Phyllis is not fanciful by nature." Betty Sue frowned. "I have never known her to raise a fuss over anything."

Star thought the idea of stealing flowers was silly.

"So someone plucks a few blooms off her bushes."

"Not some," Betty Sue corrected. "She told me there is not a single flower left in her garden."

Jenny had a random thought.

"Has anyone actually seen these flowers? I mean, does she even have a garden?"

Jason came to the woman's rescue.

"Phyllis is known for her green thumb. My mother used to beg her for cuttings and a sample of the special manure she uses on her roses. It's a closely guarded formula."

Jenny told them about her conversation with Paddy.

"He's kind of exhausting."

Betty Sue thought Jenny should give up the idea of hiring a decorator. She had taken an instant dislike to Shirley, alluding to her lack of character.

"I didn't know this was the woman you were meeting today. Listen to me, Jenny. The Cohens have a kid in some fancy school up north, learning about upholstery and stuff. He'll do the job for half the money."

This was news to Jenny. She promised to consider it, always ready to encourage a youngster.

"Shirley may be leaving Pelican Cove soon."

Betty Sue thought it was a sure sign of guilt. Paddy was getting ready to flee the scene, now that Phyllis had accused him in front of the whole town.

"Either that," Jenny mused. "Or she told me a white lie, to push me to hire her soon."

Molly thought there was another possibility.

"She plans to dump him."

Chapter 3

J enny drove to the café two days later, humming a tune to herself. The sun was just rising and the sky was clear with not a cloud in sight. The weather forecast promised a bright and sunny day with occasional gusts.

Since there wasn't much of a rush, Jenny tried to pander to the tastes of her local customers. She knew exactly what each of them favored. The cold weather meant most would crave a warm breakfast. Her first order of the day was to start a pot of oatmeal. She made it decadent by topping the individual bowls with cream, dried fruit and a special spice blend. Then she started mixing batter for pancakes.

A loud tapping sounded on the door just as she poured herself a cup of coffee. Curious, she went forth to open the door.

"Captain Charlie!" she exclaimed. "You're early."

The old salt stood shivering outside, dressed in a flannel shirt with no hat or coat, rubbing his hands to warm himself.

"Come in, come in."

"I hope you don't mind, Jenny. Guy from the city wants to go for a spin before he leaves today. Has an urgent meeting he can't miss."

Jenny assured him it was not a problem.

"Don't be a stranger. Let me fix you some coffee. You can drink that while I make pancakes."

Captain Charlie opted to sit in the kitchen while Jenny cooked. He told her the latest gossip. The winter festival was becoming a hot button issue.

"Seems foolhardy if you ask me. We already have too many festivals. There's hardly any time to put our feet up and breathe."

Jenny agreed with him. Hadn't they just wrapped up the food drive?

Half an hour later, after a hearty meal of pancakes, bacon and eggs, Captain Charlie was ready to leave.

"This will set me up for the day. Thanks Jenny."

The regulars started streaming in after that. Jenny picked up more opinions about the proposed festival, chuckling at the different arguments.

"Are you trying out any warm desserts?" A woman who worked at the library with Molly asked. "Something to go with lunch, maybe?"

Jenny promised to give it some thought. She had been experimenting with a flan recipe, inspired by her favorite Mexican restaurant in the city. Her first few attempts had not been great and she was disheartened. Then she had taken up the renovation project and forgotten all about it.

"Actually, I am working on something." She shrugged. "It will be on the menu soon."

Maybe she could introduce it for the grand reopening. Her mouth fell open when she realized what she was thinking. What would Jason say about holding a small party to celebrate the renovation?

Jenny forced herself to focus on the present. She would have to jump through plenty of hoops before that could happen. Betty Sue came in, accompanied by Heather and Jenny sighed. How much of a hurdle were her friends going to be?

"Hello ladies!" she greeted, noting the surly expression Heather wore.

It had become the norm lately. Jenny chose to leave her alone. She was sure it wouldn't be long before the façade would crack and Heather would bare her soul to her. At least that's how it had been since they became friends.

Betty Sue ignored the warm banana nut muffins Jenny placed on the table and took her to task.

"Have you called that Cohen kid yet?"

Jenny told her it wasn't going to work out. She had tried to contact him and was happy to learn he was in town. But he was busy working on a project for his father and didn't have time to come and meet her. She sensed he was not interested in sprucing up an old relic, as he referred to the Boardwalk Café. But she refrained from saying any of that to Betty Sue.

"Shirley has drawn up some designs. We are meeting after lunch today."

"That woman!" Betty Sue spat. "A chicken necker if there was one. I don't like the way she dresses, Jenny. Putting herself on display."

Her personal tastes in fashion had nothing to do with her work ethic, Jenny pointed out.

"On the contrary," Heather interrupted. "It's an indicator of her artistic tastes which are a bit too flamboyant, if you ask me. She'll turn the café into a garish bordello if you're not careful. Mark my words."

Jenny could almost feel Betty Sue's pulse speed up. Her health had been a concern all through winter and they were united in making sure she didn't get too excited. What was Heather doing, riling her up? Didn't she care about her grandmother?

"She'll do no such thing." Jenny flashed Heather a warning look. "We have discussed the kind of look I'm interested in. If Shirley cannot conform to that, we can look for a different decorator."

"Do you promise?" Betty Sue's lips quivered.

Jenny went around to put her hands on her shoulders, leaning down to give her an impromptu hug.

"Of course. Trust me a bit."

Molly and Star arrived, one carrying a stack of books, the other covered in a paint splattered apron.

"Sorry hon." Star apologized as she took off the dirty garment. "I got so engrossed I forgot I needed to be here."

Jenny convinced her to relax. She could handle the few people that made it to the café.

"You did miss out on some interesting conversations though."

Betty Sue wanted to know if the locals were still bickering over the proposed winter festival. She was going to veto the idea at the next town meeting and end all the speculation.

"Why?" Heather pouted. "It will be fun. There's nothing much to do and this winter is exceptionally cold."

Jenny told her she could help with the redecorating. Heather ignored her. Molly stepped in to diffuse the situation.

"I was thinking ... what about a mural in the dining room? Star can paint seascapes showcasing different parts of the island."

Betty Sue's face lit up. "Now that's an excellent idea, Molly. It allows us to highlight what a great artist Star is. And it's a way of showing tourists all the spots they can visit."

Heather was drawn in despite herself.

"They can make a great backdrop for pictures. Mandy would approve this idea."

They all started building on the idea and soon, many more suggestions were flying around. Jenny felt exhilarated, sensing her friends were finally getting on board. Molly had whipped out a small pad from her voluminous purse and was taking notes.

"Wicker furniture on the deck," Betty Sue decreed and they all nodded in unison.

"But we should use removable slipcovers so they can be washed." Star asked Molly to make a note.

Jenny glanced up at the ocean, happy at this new found accord. It was the kind of harmony that bound them together but had been missing for the past few weeks. The beach was deserted and the boardwalk was empty, except for a lone figure sauntering down it. He looked up and gave a small wave.

"What's Adam doing here?" she wondered to herself, then sat up with a jerk. "Molly, have you looked at the time?"

A small shriek sounded as Molly realized it was past noon. She gathered her books and beat a hasty retreat.

"The Sheriff's coming for lunch." Heather smirked for no reason.

Jenny rushed inside to assemble some sandwiches, glad she had already started a pot of tomato soup. Star came in to help her.

"Betty Sue's staying for lunch. She snared Adam into sitting with her."

"That's great. I hope he's not in a hurry. I'm going to need some time to grill these cheese sandwiches."

He appeared to have time on his hands, Star assured her. A couple came in and opted for just the soup. They were gone by the time Jenny assembled a platter of the gooey grilled cheese sandwiches. Like a true islander, she had liberally sprinkled them with Old Bay seasoning.

"Lunch is very simple today, I'm afraid." She winced as she set the platter before Adam. "I'll get the soup."

He told her to calm down. Grilled cheese and tomato soup was his favorite meal.

"Why don't you join us, Jenny?"

Betty Sue nodded, patting the empty chair next to her. Jenny made a few more trips inside and finally sat when she was sure they had everything they needed.

Adam tasted the soup and pronounced it was delicious.

"You have the magic touch, Jenny. I don't know how this town survived before you came to live here."

"Don't say that to Ethan," Jenny blushed, referring to his twin. "He puts his heart and soul into the Crab Shack."

The winter festival surfaced again. Adam wasn't worried about it because he was sure Betty Sue would squash the idea.

"Am I that predictable?" The matriarch of Pelican Cove grumbled.

Adam confessed he was anxious about an entirely different issue. He refused to elaborate when Betty Sue demanded to know what he meant.

"Let's hope it's just hot air. Or we might very well have a problem on our hands."

Jenny ate her soup, her thoughts far away. She had forgotten all about her meeting with Shirley. Apparently, it was mutual. The decorator was supposed to come to the café at 11 that morning with her designs but there was no sign of her. What's more, she had not called to explain her absence. Tardiness was not a virtue in Jenny's book.

"What's the matter, sweetie?" Star quizzed, perceptive of her moods. "Your food's getting cold and I wager your thoughts are somewhere else."

Jenny wasn't crazy about sharing what she was thinking, especially since there was no love lost between Shirley and her friends. But she couldn't hold herself back.

"The designer's late! Is that how it's gonna be?"

Betty Sue surprised her by giving Shirley the benefit of the doubt.

"She'll turn up. We had a fruitful discussion ourselves, didn't we? I say it was time well spent."

Jenny agreed with her. Adam was curious about what they were talking about. Star enlightened him.

"About time you livened up this place!" he exclaimed, drawing a frown from Betty Sue. "The lack of competition is making you take your customers for granted." He pointed at the peeling paint on a nearby pillar. "Would you enter a restaurant that looked like this?"

With a pang, Jenny realized he was right.

"You've banished any doubts I harbored about this project, Adam. I am proud of this café! It was my lifeline when I was at a low point in my life. Now it's my turn to make it shine."

Shirley Brown entered the deck in a flurry, teetering on fancy heels with red soles. She was lugging a large folder and a portable easel.

"And shine it will, Jenny!" she panted. "I promise."

She set up the easel and began rifling through the folder. Jenny's eyes widened when Betty Sue picked up her knitting and settled deeper into her chair. Star came to her rescue.

"Let's go for a walk. I went overboard with lunch."

"You had a sandwich!" Betty Sue argued. "Not a roast with fixings."

Adam took his leave. He needed to be back at his desk to do some paperwork. Star managed to pull Betty Sue to her feet.

"All that stuff about getting our approval was poppycock then."

"You have my word," Jenny assured her. "But all in good time. This is just a preliminary meeting. Maybe I will hate what Shirley's done and reject it outright."

That cheered Betty Sue and the two ladies ambled down the steps to the boardwalk.

"You were kidding, right?" Shirley bristled. "Why waste my time if you've already decided to go with someone else?"

Jenny folded her arms and pinned her with a stern gaze.

"When I hire someone, I expect them to be on time. You were supposed to be here three hours ago."

Shirley claimed a personal crisis but didn't apologize.

"You might have called," Jenny fumed. "How do I know you have not skipped town?"

Chapter 4

Shirley Brown managed to surprise Jenny. Despite the rocky start, their meeting lasted over an hour. The drawings Shirley produced were exceptional. She had captured the essence of all that Jenny wanted. Once she was done, the café would have a fresh, contemporary look with plenty of reminders of its rich history.

Jenny wasn't convinced if Shirley was committed enough to see it through.

"I want you to give this plenty of thought. Do you really want to do this, Shirley? How do I know you will not abandon me half way and just leave?"

They had set up another meeting two days later. Jenny needed that time to get the Magnolias on board.

She sat in a hot bath after going home, anxious about the big project she was embarking on. It was going to be a battle of wits with the Magnolias. And any home improvement project meant plenty of discussion with the workers. She would have to watch everything with a hawk eye and would need help.

Heather was in a funk and Jenny wasn't sure how she would cope without her trusted lieutenant.

Jason was home early and she cooked his favorite dinner. There was roast chicken, mashed potatoes with chives and plenty of butter and a chocolate cake for dessert. She was setting the table when there were a couple of loud bangs on the front door. Betty Sue barged in, followed by Heather cradling a casserole.

"Mac and cheese." She set it on the table, her eyes lighting up when she saw the chicken. "We have invited ourselves to dinner, apparently."

Jason took their coats and pulled out a chair for Betty Sue.

"What a pleasant surprise!"

Jenny knew he was being genuine. They were always happy to have impromptu guests. But the look on Betty Sue's face suggested it wasn't a casual visit.

"Out with it. I can see you're bursting to tell us something."

She wasn't prepared for what she heard next.

"Haven't you heard? They found a dead body in one of those new houses by the bay."

Jason was setting out plates for the new arrivals. He frowned as he arranged knives and forks around them.

"Is it someone we know?"

Betty Sue told them she had no idea. One of her friends had called with the news but no more information was available.

"Where's Star?" she looked around.

"She's at Jimmy's." Jenny replied. "I guess they are having dinner at his place."

Betty Sue's eyes grew wide. She asked if Jenny was sure.

"Why would she lie to me?" With a start, she realized what Betty Sue was insinuating. "Come on ... why would Jimmy go over there?"

Not very fond of the rackety Jimmy Parsons, Betty Sue launched into a diatribe on how none of them could predict what he would do next. He might have been meeting one of his shady friends.

"Jimmy's cleaned up." Jason asserted. "You're barking up the wrong tree this time."

Heather sat at the table and picked a cucumber out of the bowl of salad.

The door opened again and Molly strode in, carrying a container they were all very familiar with.

"Are those brownies?" Heather took the box from her, her mouth twisting in a grimace at the contents.

Molly did not have any more news to impart. One of her friends had told her that the house belonged to a tourist.

"You mean it is owned by a tourist? Or a tourist had rented it for the season?" Heather demanded.

It didn't make sense because hardly anyone rented houses in Pelican Cove during the winter.

"Why don't we eat?" Jenny suggested. "It's getting late and lunch feels like it was ages ago."

The sun had set while the guests arrived. A bank of clouds covered the sky and it was quite dark outside. Jason lit the lamps in the garden and promised they could have dessert outside. He would light a fire in the pit.

There was plenty to go around since Jenny always cooked for an army. Molly had brought a hearty orzo salad with roasted sweet potatoes, almonds and little balls of mozzarella.

"Do you think this is connected to the winter festival?"

Heather didn't waste any time striking her down.

"Ridiculous!" she cackled. "Haven't we heard enough about that silly festival? What's your theory, Molls?"

She answered with a shrug, unable to hide the blush stealing over her face.

"No, no. Please elaborate. You think the people in this town are so obsessed about that festival, they have started eliminating their opposition? We all belong in a mental asylum if that's true."

Jenny told her to shut up. "No need to be unkind, Heather."

"As if we haven't heard any absurd theories from you!" Betty Sue thundered. "You apologize to Molly right now, girl."

Molly hastened to explain. She had heard some women talking about offering a few booths to people from out of town for the festival. It would provide some variety and be a draw for tourists. A tarot reader had been contacted, along with a famous barbecue joint over the state border in the Outer Banks. There was also a portrait artist who was somebody's nephew. Maybe he had rented the house where the body was found.

"What's wrong with our own barbecue?" Betty Sue was incensed. "This is the first I'm hearing about this."

"It's just gossip." Jenny soothed. "You know the younger crop always has these wild ideas. They don't mean anything."

Betty Sue wouldn't let go.

"Jason and Captain Charlie can handle the barbecue as usual. And we also have Billy."

Jenny heard some footsteps outside and Billy walked in.

"Did someone say my name?"

He greeted everyone and pulled up a chair and began serving himself.

"You don't mind, Jenny? I could smell this chicken a mile away. My car drove itself here to enjoy this hearty meal."

Jenny had been talking to her son as she cooked. She was sure he had told Billy about the chicken.

"So what's this buzz about a dead body?" Billy cut his chicken, speared a piece and plunged it into the mashed potatoes. "Any theories about what happened?"

They admitted they knew nothing.

"I was at the Rusty Anchor earlier." Billy tasted the orzo and complimented Molly. "Eddie Cotton told me the bloke was ill. Probably came here to die."

Jenny warned him to stop being frivolous.

"None of your crazy ideas, Billy. He might have been a stranger to us but surely he deserves some respect?"

Billy shook his head as he took another bite. Jenny always thought the worst of him.

"I don't joke about death. It's not that farfetched, actually. This is a beautiful place, with the kind of calm a man in the twilight of his life might cherish."

Jason agreed with him. It was like going into hospice. The man opted for peace and quiet and a house with a great view.

"And what? He sat staring at the Chesapeake Bay every day, waiting for death to come and claim him?"

Jenny thought the discussion had become too morbid. She tried to change the subject.

"This mac and cheese is exceptional, Betty Sue. And I still haven't guessed your secret ingredient."

That drew a smile from the octogenarian. Her face had turned pale as Billy waxed on about his outlandish theory.

Jason stepped out and lit the logs in the fire pit. Billy started clearing the table. Heather usually helped him but Jenny wasn't surprised to see her go outside.

"Are you still not talking?" she asked Billy.

"I've tried." His shoulders slumped. "She's not ready. Where have I gone wrong, Jenny? Tell me what I've done to make her act like this?"

They asked Molly if Heather had confided in her. She shook her head.

"Billy and I will wash the dishes, Jenny. You go out and take a load off."

Heather was warming her hands over the fire when Jenny went out. She wore a cotton dress and no sweater.

"Why are you dressed for spring?" Jenny quizzed but did not get a response.

She was worried about Heather. It was clear she was going through some kind of crisis. Usually vocal about the slightest thing that bothered her, Jenny was surprised she hadn't opened up. Maybe she would prefer talking to a professional. She made up her mind to bring it up.

"Don't you have any theories?" Heather needled Jason. "A seasoned lawyer like you?"

He obliged her by offering one.

"It could be a suicide, I suppose. Man came to a remote place, away from his family for whatever reason. He might have been depressed and talked himself into doing the deed."

Heather clapped her hands in approval.

"I think you're right. He couldn't handle the deceit."

She stared at Jenny when she said that. The censure in her eyes pierced Jenny like a bullet. What did she mean?

A loud clang announced the new arrivals. Captain Charlie sauntered in, holding a plastic bag. Jenny greeted him with a small cry.

"Is that cheesecake from the Steakhouse?"

Captain Charlie nodded, handing over the bag to her with a grin. He had an ongoing arrangement with Pelican Cove's fancy restaurant. He provided them with the freshest catch and they allowed him to order anything he wanted off their menu.

"Is that all you got," Jason asked. "Or have you also brought a side of scuttlebutt?"

All eyes were trained on him, eager to hear the gossip from the docks and seafood market.

"Oyster man from Exmore says he saw a guy being shot on a boat. Smugglers from the south. They dumped his body ashore."

"Then how did it end up in that house?" Heather challenged. "I'm sorry Captain Charlie, but this story doesn't hold water."

They all agreed it was the most outlandish they had heard all evening.

Betty Sue declared it was time to eat cake. There was no more talk of the dead man after that. Jenny urged everyone to have a second helping and started a fresh pot of coffee. Two hours later, she gave the kitchen counter a final swipe with the wash cloth, feeling the exhaustion creep in. Jason was watching television in the living room.

She sat beside him and laced up her sneakers, forcing herself to go for her walk. It was a regimen she tried to stick to, no matter how busy or tired she was.

"Coming?" she asked Jason.

He didn't want to budge from his comfy spot on the couch.

The wind had picked up in the past half hour. Jenny took deep breaths and filled her lungs with the fresh, salty air. It was the best part of Pelican Cove according to her. She would never trade it for the smog of the city again.

Any doubts she may have had about stepping out disappeared after a few steps. Jenny ambled down the beach at a comfortable pace, wondering if she would run into Adam. A furry body smacked into her that instant and she got her answer.

"Tank!" she fondled the yellow Labrador she had fallen in love with. "You darling. Look what I got."

She waved the small stick she had picked up on the beach before him and threw it in the distance. Tank gave a joyful bark and bounded after it.

"You spoil him." Adam smiled, his hands burrowed in the pocket of his sweatshirt. "I hear you had quite the dinner party."

Jenny laughed.

"Does anything ever stay secret in this town?"

Adam's face turned serious and she knew he was thinking about the dead man.

"So?" she questioned. "Did that man come here to die? Or was he murdered offshore and dumped in our town?"

With a sigh, Adam told her she would have to be patient.

"I can't say anything right now, Jenny. But I might have something to share tomorrow morning."

That meant the police had not established the identity of the victim, Jenny surmised. They walked toward Seaview and bid each other goodnight.

"See you at breakfast, Adam."

Chapter 5

J enny slid a tray of blueberry muffins in the oven and went outside, nimbly going down the steps to the beach. She liked to savor her first cup of coffee, watching the sun rise over the water. It wasn't always possible in the tourist season but winter offered some solace.

The bench she sat on had been her friend Petunia's favorite. For the first time since she undertook the renovation project, her mind flooded with doubt. What would Petunia have wanted? Was she really erasing the kind woman's memory by repainting walls and fixing broken tiles?

Jenny vowed to put up a life size portrait of her friend at the entrance. That would ensure that every person coming in thought of her. Betty Sue would not be able to find any find fault with the idea. Her face lit up, believing she had found the perfect solution for her problem. There was a spring in her step as she went back to the kitchen, ready to begin her day.

Captain Charlie arrived, looking like he had a bee in his bonnet.

"Good morning," Jenny greeted him.

She had begun to feel a bit awkward around him lately. Any minute, he would mention the renovation and issue a litany of complaints. He was one of Petunia's oldest customers and had been frequenting the café since he was a child.

"Something wrong?" His bushy eyebrows drew together. "You have been awful quiet lately, Jenny."

The café was empty and it was still early. Jenny decided to take the opportunity and broach the subject with him.

"I don't know if you've heard, Captain Charlie." She waved a hand around and bit her lip, trying to choose the right words. "The café's a bit rundown."

"It looks like a dump, honey. I would've said something long ago but I didn't want to hurt you. Petunia was talking to some decorator in Onancock when she died. It was all so sudden."

They both grew sober at the painful memory.

"That's what I'm doing now." Jenny admitted. "Betty Sue is against it."

"Don't you listen to that old trout. She just likes to throw her weight around. Haven't you realized that by now?"

He cackled without any guilt since he had known the woman for several decades, unlike Jenny, who was still a bit in awe of her.

"I'm trying to bring her around."

Captain Charlie asked how he could help. He pulled up a chair and noticed its leg wobbled alarmingly. They both laughed. Jenny went in and poured two cups of coffee. Captain Charlie sat at another table. He pointed at the chair in front of him, assuring her it was in good condition.

"The café will have to be closed for a few days at the very least. I'm trying hard to minimize that period. But I'm worried about you."

He would make do with having breakfast out of a box. Jenny saw he wasn't very keen on the idea.

"Tell you what." She smiled. "You can come to Seaview and eat with us."

He gave a sheepish grin, admitting that had been his plan all along.

"But I'm not the only one who depends on the café for breakfast. There's a few old geezers like me and some ladies too. None of them would have a hot meal if it wasn't for the Boardwalk Café."

Jenny realized he was right. She would have to find a way to feed them.

"Maybe I can pack their breakfast and deliver it."

They both agreed the idea had merit. Jenny felt a load lift off her shoulders.

"Now that we have got that straightened out, tell me what you would like for breakfast. Scrambled eggs? Crab omelet?"

Captain Charlie glanced at the clock and shook his head. He had to leave in a few minutes. Jenny packed a large cup of coffee and two muffins for him, asking if he craved anything in particular for lunch.

"No doubt the whole town will be out in droves, talking about that dead body. Adam's promised to give me the scoop later today."

Captain Charlie's mouth dropped open.

"My memory's not what it used to be. I came in meaning to tell you this, Jenny."

He had run into another sailor on the way to the café that morning and learned the identity of the dead man.

"You'll never guess who the dead guy is!"

Jenny urged him to continue.

"That guy from the town hall meeting. The one who adopted a holier than thou attitude and claimed he was innocent."

"Do you mean the one that Betty Sue's friend was railing at? The man who steals flowers?"

Captain Charlie nodded, his brows raised in wonder.

"What are the odds? He's branded a thief one moment, and drops dead the next."

Jenny tried to picture the old woman from the meeting. A lined face with thinly plucked brows flashed before her. She couldn't remember the name though.

"Do you know her?"

"Phyllis Tross." Captain Charlie supplied. "Worked as a toll operator at the booth down in Cape Charles, the one at the entrance of the Chesapeake Bay Bridge-Tunnel. Used to be quite laid back. Lost her husband a few years ago, poor girl. Never knew her to be so aggressive."

But did he believe her allegations, Jenny wondered. Captain Charlie told her they sounded plausible. Phyllis would not make such claims lightly.

Jenny's mind raced forward. Although in her seventies, Phyllis Tross had appeared quite spry. Her voice had reached the corners of the town hall without the aid of a microphone. Nothing about her seemed frail. Could she have attacked her neighbor in a fit of anger? With a start, Jenny realized how fantastic her thoughts were. She had no idea how the man died.

"I can see what you're up to, Miss Jenny." Captain Charlie chuckled. "My life on the water has taught me one thing. Anything's possible."

He said goodbye after that parting shot and walked out, a smile painted on his face.

Two old ladies came in, a mother-daughter duo Jenny liked. A stream of people arrived after that and Jenny stayed busy, pouring coffee and making eggs to order. She planned to make bean soup for lunch, with macaroni and cheese.

Molly and Betty Sue came in, engrossed in some debate over Heather. Jenny was relieved it was time to take a break.

She started a fresh pot of coffee and placed muffins on a plate. Star peeped in to say hello and asked her to hurry up. She had probably skipped breakfast.

The Magnolias were engrossed in talking about the dead man when Jenny went out to the deck. She wasn't surprised. The jungle patrol must be in overdrive. No doubt one of Betty Sue's cronies had apprised her about the latest tidbit.

"At least this will put any talk of the winter festival to rest," Star proclaimed. "Bullet dodged, huh?"

Molly thought the comment was in poor taste, since they didn't know how the man had died. What if someone had come and shot him?

"I'm sure she didn't mean it like that, Molls." Jenny rushed to her aunt's rescue. "Neither of us knew this guy. Or did you? Is there something you're hiding from us?"

That sent Molly in a huff. Star told them to stop bickering.

"Do we know anything more?"

Jenny mentioned Phyllis Tross. She trained her eyes on Betty Sue and asked the question uppermost in her mind.

"How crazy is your friend about flowers?"

Betty Sue pulled out a ball of pink wool and began tying it in knots on a needle. At least that's what Jenny thought she was doing. Knitting had never been her strong point.

"Phyllis names every bush in her garden. She once said her children might have moved to the city and deserted her. But her plant babies would be with her forever."

She launched into an account of a flower show some years earlier. Phyllis had not been pleased when her prized rose did not win. She accused her opponent of stealing clippings from her garden and they had come to blows.

"Neither of them was ready to back down," Betty Sue smirked. "Phyllis pushed this woman so hard, she lost her balance and fell into the pond."

All those doubts Jenny had harbored since the morning felt justified.

"That means Phyllis Tross is violent!"

Betty Sue's eyes narrowed. She was smart enough to figure out where Jenny was going.

"You think she killed a man for stealing her flowers?"

Star and Molly set their coffee down and stared at Jenny.

"I'm sorry. I don't know your friend that well."

With a shrug, Betty Sue declared that anything was possible. But she thought it was a moot point. Jenny was jumping ahead without any solid information.

"Do you know for sure that this man was murdered?"

Star asked what they thought about the new restaurant coming up in town. It was news to everyone. They forgot about the dead man for a while and wondered what kind of cuisine the new eatery would offer.

"I hope it's something exotic, like Thai food," Molly exhaled.

The group broke up after some time and Star helped Jenny prepare lunch. A few people called in to inquire about the menu, excited about the macaroni and cheese.

"You better make two large pans," Star warned. "Mrs. Wilson was grumbling about how you haven't made it even once this winter."

The bright morning had turned gray with the arrival of thick clouds. There was a gale warning but the rain was not going to keep the hardy locals in their homes.

Jenny grated several blocks of cheddar, gouda and Swiss cheese and filled her giant pasta pot with water, setting it to boil. She called Jason's office, hoping he was free for lunch.

"Are you really making mac and cheese, darling?"

"I'll save you some." Jenny laughed and hung up.

Star commented on Heather's absence. Betty Sue had told her she was in bed, managing to alarm Jenny.

"Is she ill?"

She made up her mind to drop by the Bayview Inn on her way back home.

The customers began to troop in and filled the café. Jenny picked up a few snatches of conversation as she served them.

As expected, the recent death was on everyone's lips. Speculation was rife and wild theories abounded. Jenny heard some they had learnt last night, like the dead man being a smuggler who was killed offshore. She just smiled when people threw questions at her and kept her lips sealed.

Jason came in when the crowd thinned. Star took over the cash register and persuaded Jenny to eat with him.

"How's your day been?" he asked her, taking a big bite. "This is delicious, as usual."

Jenny ate some soup and told him about Heather. The Magnolias were growing concerned about her.

"Do you think we should take her to a therapist?"

"Honey, she's a grown woman. You can put the idea to her but she will have to walk there herself."

They needed to get her on board but who was going to broach the subject? The only guy who was capable of convincing Heather was Billy. That was not much help since Jenny suspected he was the root cause of what was ailing her.

Jason promised to think about it and left, sure he was going to nod off during his appointment.

Adam arrived just as Jenny dug her spoon into a small serving of the macaroni.

"You're holding out!" His tone was full of reproach but his eyes twinkled with mirth.

Jenny fixed a plate for him and urged Star to join them. The café was finally empty and they could linger over their meal.

None of them spoke much while they ate. Finally, Adam set his fork down and leaned back in his chair.

"Thank you for your patience. Bring 'em on, Jenny."

She shared everything she had heard about the dead man. Adam laughed at some of the theories but confirmed the victim was indeed the flower thief.

The only fact he could confirm was he had not died a natural death.

Jenny sat up in her chair, her eyes bright with excitement.

"So this is murder? Who's your top suspect?"

Chapter 6

Jenny cleaned up and prepped for the next day. Betty Sue called, asking Star to accompany her somewhere.

"She's being very closemouthed about it." Star hung up the kitchen phone, stifling a yawn. "I was looking forward to a nap."

"I'm sure she wants to meet up with her cronies to exchange some gossip. Should be a lot more invigorating than a nap." Jenny teased. "I'm almost done with my chores. Shirley will be here any minute."

Star left and Jenny went out and sat on the deck, putting her feet up on a chair. Her shoulders were sore and she stretched her arms above her head, wishing Jason was around to rub them for her.

The beach was deserted, save for the occasional hardy soul who had ventured for a stroll. A light drizzle began to fall and the sky darkened further. All Jenny wanted was to go home, snuggle under a blanket and sip a cup of hot tea with honey in it. Was that her way of putting off the renovation project?

Maybe her mind was telling her something. But no, it was high time something was done. The cafe needed a face lift. She owed it to the steady stream of customers who visited from far and wide.

Half an hour passed. Jenny sat up with a start, realizing she must have dozed off. There was no sign of Shirley. Jenny was beginning to lose her patience with the woman. Clearly, she had no concept of punctuality. Either she was not interested in the Boardwalk Café project, or she just didn't have a good work ethic. It was beginning to look like she was not a good choice.

With a sigh, Jenny realized she needed to explore more options. She would have to look up other designers on the Eastern Shore. Billy had used someone for the house he bought last year. She would wait for five more minutes. If Shirley turned up, she would get her marching orders.

The phone in the kitchen began to ring. Jenny dashed in and managed to answer before the caller hung up. It was Molly.

"I'm getting off early. You wanted to meet to finalize the designs, right? I can be there in ten minutes."

Jenny explained her designer was absconding. They didn't really have any designs to review. Molly must have sensed her frustration.

"I'm coming over anyway."

Jenny gave a shrug, then realized Molly couldn't see her.

"Sure! You're welcome anytime, Molls."

She hung up and opened the refrigerator, rooting around for a snack. The phone trilled again. Who could it be now?

"Jenny!" a hoarse voice inquired, then broke down into sobs.

"Shirley, is that you? I have been waiting for the past hour. You're late!"

The sobs intensified, followed by a keening sound. Jenny's temper deflated, replaced by concern.

"Are you sick, Shirley? That's okay, we can meet some other time. Have you been to the doctor yet?"

The sobs were replaced by sniffling.

"It's over. What am I going to do, Jenny?"

"Blow your nose and begin again, Shirley. I can't understand a single word you're saying."

Her calm but firm tone did the job.

"Paddy's gone. Murdered in cold blood. Haven't you heard, Jenny?"

"What?"

For a second, Jenny's mind went blank. Then she connected the dots. Everyone had been talking about the dead man all day but hardly anyone had mentioned him by name. Paddy Benson. He was Shirley's partner, of course. She rushed to offer her condolences.

"I'm sorry, Shirley. I didn't realize. You have my deepest regrets."

"Will you help me, Jenny? Everyone says you're this hotshot sleuth, like Nancy Drew. I need you to find out who killed my Paddy."

How could she refuse her outright? She offered to meet and talk about it. Shirley told her she needed some time to grieve. They would meet once she had a handle on her emotions and could talk for two minutes without tearing up.

Jenny returned to the deck and sat at a table, holding her head in her hands. She was having a hard time trying to collate all the facts. The gossip all day had repeatedly referred to the flower thief. Jenny thought back to the town meeting. She had scarcely paid any attention when Phyllis Tross had accused the man for stealing flowers. Yes, she had pointed at a man in the crowd and she had heard him protest. Later, Shirley introduced her to Paddy Benson. He was such a charmer, she had been engrossed in his story. At that time, she overlooked the fact that he was the same man Phyllis had been pointing at.

Jenny looked around and couldn't help smiling as she thought of the plans Paddy had proposed. He had been vehement about making the Boardwalk Café a household name across the country. Although she wasn't entirely in favor of the idea, the grand plans he outlined had given her the glimpse of what was possible. She had stored it at the back of her mind.

If there came a time when she wanted to spread her wings, she could act on some of his advice. And yes, she had made up her mind to hire Paddy as a consultant if she ever took that step.

Molly hailed her from the beach and came up at a leisurely pace. Jenny brought her up to speed.

"Paddy Benson's dead?" She looked shocked. Like Jenny, she had not made the connection. Nobody had mentioned the victim by name since yesterday. "He was a frequent guest at the library. We invited him for story hour with the kids. I'll tell you, Jenny, he had a certain way of speaking and doing voices. Held everyone spellbound."

"Shirley is devastated. I don't think she will be in a state to handle the redecoration project."

They only had a small window of time at their disposal. Once the Valentines' weekend came up, there wouldn't be a lull in the tourists until next winter. Molly thought they needed to pivot.

"What about the Cohens? Forget that kid Betty Sue mentioned. We can still hire the company to do some work."

Jenny thought she had a point.

"And the designs?"

Molly brushed off her concerns.

"You have a librarian at your disposal. Why don't you take advantage of my super powers?" She flashed a cheeky grin. "I can pull all the reference books we need. What's more, I already know where to look."

She admitted doing some research when she had spruced up her own house a few months ago.

"I've been browsing on the web too," Jenny confessed. "Some ideas are taking shape. Actually, we already know what we don't want. I think I can visualize the new space now. But I will still need plenty of help."

Molly promised to be available.

"So it's final, then. We can ask Star to do some drawings. This is great, Jenny. We can capitalize on our strengths and make this a labor of love. Betty Sue will be thrilled, you'll see."

What about timelines, Jenny asked. She told Molly about Shirley's request.

"You don't owe her anything. Jenny, we barely know the woman."

She was right, of course. But Jenny couldn't stop thinking about Paddy.

"He was so full of praise for the café. Molly, he outlined a business plan for expansion and promised there would be a Boardwalk Café in every beach town along the east coast if I followed his advice."

Molly squeezed her hand and lifted one shoulder in a shrug.

"Let's call Heather and go for a drive."

Jenny let herself be talked into it. A change of scene sounded appealing. She went in to powder her nose and came out, slinging her bag over her shoulder.

Shirley paced the deck, her face blotchy and hair in disarray. Jenny was shocked to see she wore a faded tee shirt over flannel pajamas. They were pink with little kittens on them.

Molly's eyes followed the woman, her brows raised in consternation.

"Hello Shirley!" Jenny greeted her. "I thought you weren't coming until tomorrow."

The woman whirled around and leaped into Jenny's arms, hugging her tight. Jenny waited a few seconds before giving her a gentle nudge.

"I am sorry for your loss."

"Paddy will be missed." Molly joined in. "He was a favorite with us library workers."

Shirley's eyes shimmered with tears. She pulled a tissue out of the dispenser on the table and crumpled it, then remembered to dab her eyes.

"Shall we begin?" she asked Jenny. "You said you had some questions for me."

Her knees gave out and she seemed to stumble. Jenny caught her just in time.

"When was the last time you ate anything?" she questioned, pushing her down in a chair. "I am going to fix us all some coffee. We can talk after that."

Shirley obeyed without question.

"I'll do whatever you say. Paddy was my guardian angel, Jenny. I can't understand why anyone would hurt him."

Chapter 7

Jenny plied Shirley with cookies. The woman gave in and nibbled on one. Her pale, tear streaked faced got some color after she drank her coffee. Jenny was glad to see her revive a bit.

"Tell me about Paddy." Jenny invited, running a hand through her hair.

She wanted to be sensitive, but she needed to learn about the victim if she was to be any help.

"How long have you known him?"

They met nine years ago. She had been at a loose end. Jenny noted Shirley didn't say much about that.

"I signed up for a group hike, the kind organized by those outdoor sports companies. It was in the Smoky Mountains. A four day hike with guides and everything arranged for us."

Paddy had been a part of the group. Within hours, it was clear he was the leader of the pack. He set everyone at ease, drawing a smile from the most grouchy member.

"We had to hike ten miles every day, you know," Shirley reminisced. "I was recovering from the flu and also completely out of shape. The guide spotted that right away and suggested I turn back. But Paddy intervened."

His kindness made an impression. When she slipped down a riverbed on the second day and scraped her knee, he made sure she got first aid. Then he carried her over his shoulders until their next halt.

"At first, I thought he was odd. That accent is really hard to understand. He had a wild look about him, with shoulder length hair and eyes that darted everywhere. I asked what he was afraid of."

"And?" Jenny prompted.

Paddy had just arrived in the country after selling most of his assets in Australia. It was a dream he had cherished since his youth, when he visited California and hiked the Joshua Tree Park. He had always wanted to come back.

"Life on a cattle station is hard." Shirley was emphatic. "The poor man had such a rough life. His wife couldn't handle it and walked out a few years after marriage. He promised his Pa he would hold on to their ancestral ranch."

Paddy's parents passed and he found he was on the wrong side of sixty. It was high time he did something for himself. The old wanderlust had surfaced and he recollected the promise young Paddy had made to himself.

"Here I am, the man declared, spreading his arms wide." Shirley sighed. "The sun was setting over the ice capped Smokies behind him. I couldn't help it, Jenny. I fell in love."

Paddy didn't really have a home to go back to after the trek. He followed Shirley to her town and took a room in a motel. A month later, they decided they couldn't live without each other and opted for a fresh start.

"I love the ocean." Shirley glanced at the water before them. "And we also wanted to be close to the mountains. We saw a brochure about the Eastern Shore at one of those visitor centers you have at the state border. Paddy suggested we come down for a drive."

They had checked out a few towns in the area and settled on Pelican Cove.

"This place is my home now and I can't imagine living anywhere else."

Molly had been quiet while Shirley narrated the story of her life. She stepped in with the questions Jenny had been hesitating to ask.

"When did you marry him?"

Shirley's nostrils flared and she stared at Molly.

"Who is this? I thought you would leave once I began to speak. Do you always stick around and poke your nose in other people's business?"

Jenny didn't care for this verbal attack on her friend.

"You know Molly, don't you? She's my best friend. You don't have to worry about her."

Shirley objected. Anything she had said was in the strictest confidence.

"My friends are closer to me than family." Jenny's voice held a note of warning. "I share everything with them. And they are an immense help to me in solving any crime."

With a shrug, Shirley looked away but didn't apologize. Jenny opened her mouth to object but Molly caught her eye and gave a slight shake of her head.

Realizing she had many more questions for Shirley, Jenny took the hint.

"This is the tough part. Did Paddy get into a fight with anyone? In short, did he have any enemies?"

Shirley mentioned the town meeting.

"You were there, right? So you are aware how that crazy woman was railing at him. She turned up at our doorstep every day to give Paddy an earful."

Jenny asked if there was any truth in her allegations. Shirley deftly sidestepped the question.

"Phyllis Tross is a menace. She was determined to drive us out of town because she claims Paddy insulted her."

"Or was it because you were ..." Molly interrupted. "You know."

"I know what you're getting at, okay? And no, that was not the reason. That old biddy had some ridiculous idea of building a website to sell the flowers from her garden. She approached Paddy to create a business plan for her. He did a study and told her the idea was not feasible."

Phyllis took it as the ultimate insult and began her vendetta against Paddy after that. Shirley had pleaded with him to come up with something nominal to please the woman. But he claimed he couldn't go against his convictions.

"He said he couldn't advise the woman to invest her hard earned money on an idea that had no merit. Phyllis was on a fixed income and would lose any little savings she had. My Paddy was looking out for her, actually. But she refused to see that."

Jenny had never imagined anyone would make such a fuss over flowers. Who was Phyllis Tross planning to sell her flowers to? Almost every home in Pelican Cove boasted a well kept garden. It was a matter of pride for all of them. Some hired gardeners, others toiled themselves, but they managed to make the flowers bloom all year round.

"The police are already looking into this, Shirley. Adam Campell, our Sheriff, is very capable. I'm sure they will have an update for you very soon."

Shirley began to shake her head.

"No, no. That's not what I've heard. They say he doesn't take any action without consulting you first. Look, Jenny. Name your price. Paddy put a certain amount in my savings account every month for my personal expenses."

She pointed a hand in the direction of her silhouette. No doubt she was referring to her expensive clothes and designer shoes.

"What I mean is, I am not lacking in resources." She looked around, her eyes gleaming as a thought struck her. "And the redecoration. I won't charge you a cent."

Jenny thanked her but told her it wasn't necessary. She had helped a friend or two in the past but wasn't looking to make any money.

"Don't you consider me a friend?"

Molly twisted her mouth and shook her head. Jenny saw her from the corner of her eye and tried to remain stoic. Shirley was being too pushy.

"Let me think about it." Jenny would not commit more than that. "But there's one thing. You will have to be open, Shirley. Tell me about your relationship."

Shirley's cheeks turned pink and it was obvious she was going to launch into a tirade again. Jenny warded her off.

"How well did you get along with Paddy? How often did you argue?"

"Never! He was a lamb, my poor Paddy."

Molly's face held a look of disbelief.

"It's okay, Shirley," Jenny soothed. "Couples bicker over silly things. It's perfectly normal. I'd rather know so I'm not caught unawares."

"Nothing like that. He was very easy going. That's the Australian in him, I guess."

It was time to break up the meeting. Jenny would contact her if she needed any more information. Shirley left the way she had come, walking down the boardwalk.

"We don't know where she lives," Molly quipped.

They did, Jenny corrected. Phyllis Tross was Paddy's next door neighbor. It would be easy enough to ask Betty Sue about the location.

"Are we meeting at the Rusty Anchor?"

"I'm not sure. Maybe we should go to the Bayview Inn and see what Heather's up to."

They prepared themselves to be turned away. Heather was not nice to be around when she was in a temper.

Betty Sue greeted them at the door and shook her head when Jenny raised a questioning eyebrow.

"She hasn't come out of her room all day. I fixed her a ham and pineapple sandwich like I did when she was a kid. She used to gobble it down when she came from school."

Betty Sue had knocked on the door and left the plate outside.

"Food is one thing Heather cannot live without." Jenny took a deep breath and started up the stairs, Molly close behind.

They came to a halt outside Heather's room. The plate Betty Sue mentioned was nowhere to be seen.

"What did I tell you?" Jenny whispered and started banging on the door.

"Heather!" Molly hailed. "Stop acting like a child and open the door."

Footsteps sounded and came closer. The door opened a crack. Heather spotted them and slammed the door again.

"She doesn't want to see me." Jenny folded her arms. "Do you think I'm the one she's mad at?"

They tried to reason with Heather for a few minutes but had to give up. Jenny was pensive as they trudged down the stairs in defeat. Betty Sue sat in the living room, knitting something in a frenzy. She glanced up, her eyes full of despair.

"She ate the sandwich," Molly reassured her. "Don't worry, Betty Sue. However many tantrums Heather throws, she won't starve herself."

Jenny sat down with a thud.

"We have been under a misconception. Billy's not the one she's mad at. It's me!"

Betty Sue and Molly both stared back, their mouths open in astonishment.

"What makes you think that, dear?"

Jenny wracked her brain but could not come up with a solid response.

"I'm as much in the dark as you are. Heather will have to enlighten me."

That would not happen until she was ready to sit down and talk.

"We need to clear the air somehow. Why don't we set up a spa night and have a kind of intervention?"

Heather would never agree to one in her current mood, Molly reasoned. And she would walk out the moment they tried to gang up on her.

"We have to do something," Betty Sue cried. "I say we try this."

Jenny promised to set it up and invited her for dinner. Heather could sulk as much as she wanted. Her behavior was having a detrimental effect on her grandmother's health and they needed to avoid that.

Betty Sue hesitated for a minute, then agreed to go to Seaview with Jenny. Billy drove up when they stepped out of the house.

"Any chance I can talk to her?" He sounded hopeful.

"You can try!" Betty Sue let him hug her and patted his arm.

Jenny offered to take Molly home. They rode in silence for a few minutes, lost in their thoughts.

"What do you fancy for dinner?" Jenny asked.

Molly distracted her by slapping her hand on the dashboard.

"Oh wow! She's sly as a fox." Molly's eyes hardened. "I know you feel sorry for Shirley, Jenny. But I think she's trying to manipulate you."

Jenny answered with a smile. "How so?"

Molly asked her to think back a couple of days. Hadn't Shirley mentioned she was planning to leave town for good? Was that with or without Paddy? If she had been scheming to dump the man, why was she playing the grieving widow now?

Chapter 8

Star was chopping vegetables for a stew when they got home. Jenny entrusted Betty Sue to her care and went up to her room. She had been longing to put her feet up. A lot had happened that day and she felt the need to be alone for a while.

Changing into some sweats and a fluffy robe, she sat in the window seat, trying to organize her thoughts. Heather took precedence over the murder. What could she have done to distress her friend?

The sun crept closer toward the water and dipped below the horizon. Golden twilight made its presence known, giving way to darkness but Jenny was none the wiser. She scarcely noticed Jason come in until he placed a hand on her shoulder and shook it.

"What's wrong?"

Jenny poured her heart out. Jason listened patiently and told her there was only one solution. She needed to have a heart to heart with Heather.

"But when?" Jenny cried.

"When she's ready." Jason shrugged. "She'll come to you. Just give her time."

Jenny declared it would be difficult to act normal as Jason suggested but she would give it a try. Savory aromas were wafting from the kitchen.

"Shall we have dinner now?" Jason teased. "Your husband is starving."

Star and Betty Sue bustled in the kitchen. Mostly, Betty Sue perched on a stool and barked orders while Star did her bidding. But the two seemed to be having a good time.

There was a bowl of pimento cheese on the counter, beside a tray of crudites and crackers. A bottle of wine was uncorked.

Jenny spread the zesty dip on a cracker and popped it in her mouth, accepting the glass Jason handed her. It was a local wine from an Eastern Shore winery. They had gone to a wine tasting session there and bought a selection to sample at home.

"What do you think?" Jason asked. "Shall we order a case?"

Betty Sue told him to go ahead and Jenny and Star agreed.

There was fresh bread to go with the stew. It was a simple, comforting meal, and it hit the spot. Dessert was vanilla ice cream with warm peaches.

Betty Sue gave a few yawns and declared she was ready to go home. Jason and Jenny drove her back to the inn.

"Shall we go for a drive?" he proposed.

Jenny was yearning to learn more about Paddy's murder. She shook her head.

"Let's go home and take a walk on the beach. That way, we can turn back whenever we want and go to bed right away."

Jason quirked an eyebrow and laughed.

"And you can run into Adam."

She saw the humor lurking in his eyes and played along.

"Yes! Unlike you, he doesn't travel out of town every few days."

Jason grew serious.

"Does it bother you? You never mentioned that before."

Jenny hastened to apologize, then admitted she didn't know where that had come from. Maybe it did irk her, deep down. Jason, the laid back small town lawyer she had married had suddenly acquired many new clients and become busy. On the other hand, Billy, the big time corporate lawyer had opted for a slow pace, determined to enjoy life before it was too late.

The night was windy and Jenny snuggled in her jacket, leaning close to Jason. It wasn't long before they encountered Adam throwing a ball for his yellow Labrador. Tank greeted Jenny with an enthusiastic bark and brushed against her, scampering off after she leaned down to give him a good rub.

Adam and Jason caught up on what some of their mutual friends were up to. They made plans to meet at the pub for a drink.

"Shirley came by the café this morning," Jenny informed Adam.

"Shirley *Brown*," Adam emphasized. "She was not married to the victim."

Jenny placed her hands on her hips and got ready to rebuke him.

"That's the kind of comment Betty Sue would make, considering her age. But I thought you lived in the twenty first century."

Adam rolled his eyes and told her she was the one with prejudice.

"You have to stop thinking the worst of me, Jenny. Pause for a minute and think about the legal repercussions."

Jason sided with Adam.

"This is complicated."

Jenny deflated and waited for one of them to explain what they meant.

"Shirley may have enjoyed the benefits of a wife while Paddy was alive," Adam said. "But she doesn't have spousal privilege. That means she is not his next of kin."

"You mean she will not inherit his money."

"That's an unknown for us at this point," Adam replied. "Paddy may have made a will, and left everything to Shirley. We are looking into it."

Jenny was sure that Shirley was grieving for Paddy and had asked for her help.

"It could be an act," Adam interrupted. "Say she's sitting on a gold mine. Of course she's not going to throw a party to celebrate her wealth."

Why would he think that, Jenny questioned. Had Shirley done anything to earn his poor opinion? She sensed his reluctance when he didn't answer right away.

"Out with it."

"Shirley Brown is a suspect. In fact, I will show all my cards and tell you right now that she is the top suspect in this investigation." He spread his hands wide. "I'm sorry, Jenny. You seem to be attached to this woman."

Jenny leapt to correct him. She barely knew Shirley and owed her nothing. Then she revealed that Molly did not have a good feeling about the woman either.

"Molly thinks she's a fake."

Jason had been quiet during this conversation. He warned Jenny to be careful.

"Promise me you won't take any unnecessary risks."

Jenny looked at Adam and broke into an impish smile. What could go wrong when the Sheriff had her back?

They were just a few paces from Seaview and Jenny invited Adam in for a drink. Jason seconded her.

Adam admitted he felt chilled to the bone and longed to warm himself before the walk back to his car.

Star had left a light on in the living room. Jason lit the logs in the fireplace while Jenny headed to the kitchen to make hot chocolate. She pulled a bar of dark chocolate from the pantry and began to chop it roughly while the milk warmed. Five minutes later, she popped marshmallows in each mug, set some cookies out on a plate, and went out.

Adam and Jason were sprawled on the couch, watching a game on TV.

"Thanks Jenny." Adam picked up a mug and took a sip. "This is delicious."

The fire crackled, filling the room with a golden glow. Jenny wrapped her hands around her mug, enjoying the warmth from the hearth.

"Phyllis Tross must be your number one suspect, if you ask me. Were you there when she accused Paddy of stealing her flowers?"

Adam gave her a knowing look. She was well aware that Adam had been at the town hall that night.

"That's a laughable motive. She might love her flowers but a petite old lady like her is not capable of stabbing a tall, hefty guy like Paddy Benson."

Jason's eyebrows shot up. So there was no doubt they were dealing with murder!

"Unless he stabbed himself, which is very hard to accomplish," Adam snorted. "No, this is very much a murder."

Not willing to give up easily, Jenny objected that Phyllis had a great opportunity to commit the crime. She lived next door to the dead man.

Adam picked up a cookie and bit into it, brushing crumbs off his chest.

"Not really." His mouth stretched into a wide grin.

"What aren't you telling me?" Jenny demanded.

She would never have guessed what Adam revealed next. Paddy Benson had not died in his own house. His body had been discovered at a different property. Shirley had not mentioned that either.

"You could have told me that before, Adam." She railed.

With a flash, she remembered the earliest reports of the crime. It had happened at a rental bungalow in an upcoming area of town. How could she have overlooked that? She pressed Adam for more information.

"Whose house was it? Anyone we know?"

He wasn't a local, Adam replied. Just a man who had invested money in the house, intending to rent it out to tourists.

"It's becoming very common now," Jason added. "People in the cities are picking up these properties as an investment, thinking the prices will skyrocket in a few years. They spend their vacations here and rent the places out for the rest of the year."

Adam confirmed this. The owner of the house lived in Washington, DC. He had come down to fix something and got a nasty shock.

"The house was sitting empty then?" Jenny queried.

Adam shook his head.

"Here's the funny thing. The owner said it was rented for the season. A man was living there but he called to complain the heat was on the fritz. He wasn't prepared to rough it out and moved to a hotel."

The police were looking into his whereabouts.

"Is it anyone we know?" Jenny asked, almost sure of the answer.

"Some random tourist," Adam sighed. "I can't tell you anything more about him."

Tank had been snoozing by the hearth. He sprang up and stretched, then trotted over to Adam.

"Time to go home, huh?"

Adam placed his mug on the tray and offered to wash it.

"No need. I'll just put them in the dishwasher."

They bid each other goodnight, Jenny imploring him to keep her posted about any new developments. Adam gave a sharp laugh and told her it was against the rules. He could not share any information about an ongoing investigation.

Jason slapped him on the back and saw him out.

"What now?" he turned around, chuckling when he saw the pout on his wife's face. "You know he's kidding."

They decided to call it a night. Jenny brushed her hair and slathered night cream on her face. It was made with collagen and guaranteed to reduce wrinkles and make her look younger. A few years ago, city dwelling Jenny would have scoured the shops for such products. But she realized the last few years in Pelican Cove had changed her. Her work at the café and the new relationships she had built meant more to her than superficial trappings.

Jason's eyes followed her around the room.

"Tough day. Best sleep on it."

Jenny walked to the thermostat to turn the heat up.

"Why would someone drive all the way from the city, just to fix the heat?"

Jason gave a deep yawn, struggling to stay awake.

"I don't know, honey. He has a new car and wanted to stretch its legs?"

"Ha ha!" Jenny frowned. "Can't he hire a local to check such things for him? I mean, the cost of gas itself ..."

She walked to the window and stared at the horizon. The scent of jasmine wafted up from the garden. Jenny couldn't wait for spring when her favorite roses would bloom, along with the gardenia.

"Put her to work," Jason mumbled, almost asleep. "Make her feel wanted, Jenny."

She didn't have to ask who he was talking about. Heather had been stalwart in her support when Jenny was new in town. Now it was her turn.

Chapter 9

Jenny was calm as she beat eggs for omelets the next morning. The muffins were ready and the vegetables were diced. She had time to sit outside and drink her coffee.

Captain Charlie came in at opening time and remarked on her mood.

"You look very chipper this morning. Have you and Heather made up?"

Jenny followed him out to the deck, holding his plate of crab omelet and toast.

"Jason and I talked. I'm not going to worry about it anymore. She knows where to find me."

Star walked up the boardwalk and joined them. Jenny tempted her with a crab omelet.

"I have to go in and start the soup."

She made the chicken salad and felt she had things under control when Star came in.

"Are you serious about that mural?"

"Of course!" Jenny chirped. "What better showcase for your work than the Boardwalk Café? The murals will entice the tourists and they are bound to have questions." She paused before proposing the idea she'd been mulling over. "You know that room with the old boxes that's been locked forever? I am thinking we will display your paintings there. People can buy them and also put in custom orders."

Star's eyes welled up.

"Do you mean that? We can put a few extra tables in there to accommodate more customers."

Jenny shook her head.

"The customers are fine. I checked the plans and it's not a big room. But it's perfect for this purpose."

Star told her the room contained Petunia's stuff. She had always kept it locked so none of them had an idea what it contained.

"Isn't it time we found out?" Jenny asked with a frown. "This doesn't mean I am not grateful, Star. But what's the harm in at least taking a look inside?"

They were mulling over this when a dry voice interrupted.

"Grandma's not going to like it. She'll make you squirm."

Jenny whirled around, unable to believe her eyes. Dressed in a pair of knee high red leather boots, Heather leaned against the wall, wearing a bored expression.

Curbing her desire to rush forward and embrace her, Jenny held back and gave a nod. Heather was bound to be skittish and there was no point in overwhelming her.

"We can go through all the stuff together and decide what's to be done. Betty Sue will agree to that."

Star wondered about the key that would open the lock. Jenny picked up the bunch of keys she carried around and waved them in front of her.

"One of these opens the front door, one's for the mailbox. I have no idea what the others are for."

Apart from two local women who were murmuring to each other over their coffee, there was no one in the café. Star declared there was no time like the present and they walked the five steps to the locked room. Jenny tried one key after another with no luck.

She looked over her shoulder and realized Heather wasn't with them. But she appeared from the kitchen, brandishing a wire of some sort.

"What's that?"

"The key that will open that door."

Star and Jenny watched, amazed, as Heather thrust the wire in the old lock and began jiggling it.

"It's rusted." She exclaimed in disgust. "But maybe ..."

There was a distinct clink and the lock snapped open. Jenny and Star clapped their hands.

"I didn't know you could pick locks." Jenny's voice was full of awe. "What other skills have you been hiding from us?"

Heather pushed the door with both hands, then gave it a kick. The door swung open suddenly. A musty odor escaped, making them cover their noses in disgust. Cobwebs hung from the ceiling.

Heather stomped in and walked around the periphery.

"Well?" she demanded, taking in their awe struck faces. "Whaddaya know?" Then she dissolved into raucous laughter.

The room was empty, except for a tiny table in one corner. It was covered in a thick layer of dust and one of its legs was missing.

Jenny could very well guess the question that would consume them for days. Why had Petunia locked an empty room?

Heather walked out, her bored expression back on her face.

"I think we're done here. Can a body get a cup of coffee around here?"

Star nudged Jenny, silently urging her to follow Heather. Jenny poured two cups of coffee and took them out to the deck.

"Have you given up sleuthing?"

Jenny gave her the rundown on everything she knew.

"Shirley's pressing me to do something but Adam thinks she's not above board. The police believe she's the top suspect."

Heather stirred her coffee, her brows set in a frown. It was obvious she did not believe that.

"Phyllis Tross is the one they should be looking at. The woman accused Paddy in broad daylight. I mean, before a whole room of suspects. Did you see the venom in her eyes? If only looks could kill ..." She took a sip of her coffee. "How did Paddy die, by the way?"

"Stabbed." Jenny informed her. "And not even in his own home."

Heather was intrigued when she learned about the rented house where Paddy's body had been discovered. It sounded like something Phyllis might think of.

"She wanted to divert attention from herself."

Jenny asked why Heather was so against the poor woman. All Heather would say was the woman had a mean streak that she kept hidden.

"Phyllis is a member of Grandma's knitting club. I have known her since I was a child. She never had a good word for me, Jenny. Told Grandma she needed to be more firm."

Jenny couldn't hide a smile. No doubt Heather had been willful while growing up. It must have grated on a lot of people. She rubbed one of the charms hanging around her neck on a chain. Her son had been a terror until he was ten. Some well meaning neighbors had made it a point to give her advice on how to control him.

"If that's her only sin ..."

Heather proposed meeting the woman.

"She's retired and spends most of her time in the garden. We'll find her home, unless she's skipped town."

They both laughed. Jenny was glad Heather hadn't lost her sense of humor. She went in and told Star about their plan.

"Go ahead, sweetie. I can handle things here."

The day was cold and wet with the occasional drizzle after a few morning showers. Jenny surmised they would be back before lunch.

The drive didn't take long. Jenny held back from asking any questions, unwilling to disturb the temporary truce. Heather munched on a stick of licorice, content with staring at the rain.

Phyllis Tross twisted her mouth in a grimace and seemed reluctant to let them in. Heather squeezed past her and went in, leaving her no choice.

"You have always been a trial for Betty Sue," she trilled. "Why are you here?"

Jenny began to introduce herself.

"No need. You're the woman who fleeced Petunia of her life's earnings."

Jenny swallowed the avalanche of guilt that swept through her. Heather came to her rescue.

"She has no use for it now, does she? Let me remind you that Petunia loved Jenny like a daughter."

Phyllis flashed her an irritated look and asked what they wanted. Heather took the lead again.

"We are here to make things easy for you, Mrs. Tross. Why not confess you killed poor Paddy? It will save the police some time and effort."

"If only ..." Phyllis clucked. "But I am glad he's gone. Good riddance! At least my garden can flourish now. The Garden Club wouldn't have chosen it as part of the Garden Walk if that goon had his way."

Did she mean Paddy, Jenny probed. Phyllis muttered under her breath and gave her a stern look.

"Of course I'm talking about that uncouth lout who was my neighbor. No manners at all. No regard for the locals. Is it any wonder he was from Australia? I hear they are all like that. Criminals!"

Jenny shrank back at her acrimonious tone.

"That's an unfair observation, Mrs. Tross. If Paddy wronged you in some way, it was his own doing."

"There is no doubt!" Phyllis grew more incensed. "Going on and on about that ranch of his. What do I care how many thousand cattle he had?"

She cared about her flowers though, Jenny hinted.

Phyllis launched into an account of how Paddy had tormented her. He was all benevolence during the day, inviting her over for a drink or appetizers.

"He invaded my garden at night, see? Cut all the blooms and displayed them in vases through his house. But that wasn't enough for the man. He flaunted them in my face."

How could she be sure the flowers came from her garden, Heather argued. He could have ordered them from a florist. The man was supposed to be loaded.

"I know my babies." Phyllis mourned. "A whole bed of daffodils, decimated! I had talked to them just before turning in the previous night. The next day, there's a big urn of daffodils in Paddy's foyer. Coincidence? I say not!"

Jenny tried to commiserate with her. Did Paddy or Shirley hold a grudge against her? Why would they trouble her so?

"That woman!" Phyllis spat. "Don't even get me started."

Heather was getting impatient.

"Did he have problems with anyone other than you? Arguments? Fights?"

Phyllis replied she was not interested in talking about the man. He had harassed her enough when he was alive. She would not spare a single thought for him anymore.

Jenny felt a tickle in her throat. The woman hadn't even offered them a drink.

"Can I get some water please?"

"Aren't we done yet?" She glared at Heather. "The kitchen's that way."

Heather shot up from her seat and went in, returning with a glass on a tray. Jenny took a few sips, eager to leave.

"Do you want to be arrested for Paddy's murder, Mrs. Tross?" Heather threatened. "You better not hide anything from us. Jenny here is a hot shot detective and the Sheriff values her opinion."

Phyllis bristled with barely concealed anger, an angry blush stealing up her cheeks.

"I think someone was keeping an eye on him. A man has been lurking around on our street, watching Paddy's house. And he followed Paddy whenever he stepped out."

Was Phyllis making him up, Jenny wondered. Heather was ahead of her.

"Tourist or local? Did you recognize him?"

"Not local." Phyllis replied quickly. "Never seen him in town before. And he wasn't at the town meeting so he's not one of those young chicken neckers who are buying houses on the island."

She confessed she had considered talking to him.

"He might have the evidence I need," she explained. "I'm sure he saw Paddy stealing my flowers because he stuck to the man like a shadow."

And they were back to the flowers. Jenny said a hasty good-bye before Phyllis could launch on her hobby horse.

"Thank you for speaking to us, Mrs. Tross. You have been a big help." She hesitated. "Why don't you come to the café for lunch sometime? My treat."

Phyllis didn't actually smile but her face softened a tiny fraction. She answered with a nod.

"What did I tell you, Jenny?" Heather crowed on the way back. "Nasty woman!"

"She's old and on her own. I think she's just a bit whimsical."

Heather shook her head, unwilling to let go.

"I thought there was something about her but I couldn't remember it earlier this morning. She was a toll booth operator at the bridge, right?"

Jenny nodded. Captain Charlie or Betty Sue had mentioned that.

"Well, she attacked a woman because she didn't have change. The police arrested her and she was found guilty." Heather's eyes sparkled with indignation. "They sent her to take anger management classes."

They reached the café and Jenny scrambled out, spotting a few customers inside. She asked Heather what she was getting at.

"Phyllis Tross is violent when provoked."

Chapter 10

Jenny found a captive audience awaiting her on the deck in the form of the Magnolias.

"Well?" Betty Sue boomed. "Did Phyllis let you in?"

Jenny marveled how her friend had the measure of every person in town. She gave a brief account of their visit, prompted by Heather.

"She didn't even offer us a drink, Grandma."

"For shame. The proprieties must be observed, no matter what. I'm going to give her a piece of my mind."

Heather was surprised. She had always thought Betty Sue had a special liking for the woman.

"You are mistaken. I don't know why Phyllis joined the knitting club. She's nothing like the rest of us. More importantly, she has no interest in knitting!"

Most of the ladies in the club knit socks and blankets for the poor and donated them. When Phyllis heard this, she had not been pleased. She told them point blank she had no interest in wasting her hard earned money on worthless people.

"She'd rather buy more plants?" Jenny guessed.

Betty Sue told her she was right. They had her measure right then. The woman continued to come to the meetings and they more or less ignored her.

"But why let her be a member?" Molly was curious. "Don't you have strict rules about who can get in?"

Jenny raised an eyebrow in question. Molly gave her a slight shrug. Apparently, Molly had tried to join them and had been denied entry.

"Age is a factor," Betty Sue was kind. "Ten more years and we might consider you, Molly. We took a vote and decided we'd let her come when she wanted. Most of us knew her mother. Phyllis was always quick to find fault. She's fought with most girls her age over something or the other and has hardly any friends."

"But can she be violent?" Jenny stressed. "Heather said she attacked someone?"

Betty Sue frowned, then sat up in her chair.

"I forgot all about that. Yes, she was obsessed about getting the exact change at the toll booth. The locals humored her but tourists were not very pleased."

Inspite of that, Betty Sue didn't see her actually taking anyone's life.

Star came out with a fresh pot of coffee and some warm muffins. Jenny thanked her and poured herself a cup, adding cream and sugar. She gave a sigh of pleasure after taking a sip.

"This is perfect. All I want to do is go home and snuggle under the covers, maybe read a good book."

It was the weather, they agreed.

"Hanging out with your dear friends is the next best thing," Heather remarked.

The others nodded, exchanging surprised glances. What had wrought this sudden change in Heather's behavior? Had she finally seen reason? Jenny hoped her largesse extended toward Billy. The poor man had been in anguish for several weeks.

They talked about the proposal for the winter festival. Ballot boxes had been placed across town, asking people to vote. But Jenny knew Betty Sue had veto powers. Personally, she wanted to move ahead with the renovation.

Molly approved the idea about displaying Star's paintings.

"It's all so exciting, Jenny. We should have done that long ago."

Jenny stole a glance at Betty Sue. She must have seen the broken lock on the room. What was her reaction to turning the room into a gallery of sorts?

"That room is the perfect size, Jenny." Betty Sue replied. "Give it a fresh coat of paint, air it out and you'll have a nice, cozy space at your disposal. Maybe you could put a table for two in there and hire it out for special occasions, like dates and stuff."

There was a stunned silence.

"You don't mind we broke the lock?" Jenny ventured. "Was that room special for Petunia? I expected to find some personal stuff inside but it's almost empty. Well, except for that broken desk."

A rumble began in Betty Sue's throat and she began to shake. Jenny was surprised to see her erupt in laughter.

"Nothing of the sort. It used to be a cloak room, back in the day. A glorified coat closet. Then Petunia used it as a pantry to store her supplies. Don't know what happened after that. Or why she put a lock on the door."

"You knew that all along?" Star was cross.

Jenny stepped in hastily before a new argument flared.

"I have been thinking, Betty Sue. You were right about getting the work done from local handymen. Molly's going to help me with the designs. In fact, we already have some ideas."

She provided a rough outline of what she had envisioned.

"Everything will be simple, designed to highlight all the art. We'll have the murals in the dining area. Any remaining portions of the wall can be white. Fresh curtains at the windows ..."

"Blue gingham," Heather supplied. "They look quaint and appropriate for a seaside café."

Jenny nodded eagerly. She had sent her thoughts to Mandy, asking for her input.

"Her advice will be valuable, since she has an idea of what the customers want."

Betty Sue was impressed.

"Asking Mandy is a stroke of genius. The girl is talented and she's never let us down. Why, we would never have won Prettiest Town in America without her."

Glad and not a bit relieved to gain Betty Sue's favor, Jenny felt a surge of energy. The Boardwalk Café would get new life come spring.

Molly had some news for them.

"Have any of you heard about the floating restaurant?"

The blank faces around her gave her the answer she sought. She darted an uncertain glance at Betty Sue.

"I heard some women talking about it in the library. One of them was visiting from somewhere up the coast. They think it will be built on a pier and will hang over the water."

"Like those bungalows in Bora Bora?" Jenny asked.

Molly nodded but Betty Sue was beginning to turn red.

"What's a boar ... what you just said."

"It's an island in the South Pacific, Grandma." Heather supplied. "But that would require a pier like structure, right? Can't be in Pelican Cove or we would have heard about it."

"Did the woman say it was going to be in Pelican Cove?" Star asked Molly.

She wasn't sure. The snatches of conversation she heard were vague and the only words that had registered on her mind were floating and restaurant.

Building another pier would require plenty of time and money but mostly, Jenny wasn't sure if it was doable. Pelican Cove was a barrier island. Several chunks of it had broken off during a great storm.

"Is it even feasible?" she quizzed. "What about all the shoals?"

Betty Sue thought it was all moot. If anyone was thinking of building a pier in Pelican Cove, she would be the first to know about it.

The phone in the kitchen began to ring. Jenny sprang up and went in. She also wanted to check on the soup. Her caller prompted her to step out again.

"It's for you, Betty Sue. Sounds like Phyllis Tross, although she refused to identify herself."

Betty Sue shuffled in and picked up the receiver. Jenny saw red spots appear on her face as her chest heaved with emotion. She slammed the receiver, looking as dark as the clouds that lined the midmorning sky.

Jenny urged her to calm down. Betty Sue allowed her to lead her back to the deck.

"That woman has a lot of gall."

"Phyllis?" Star wanted to confirm. "What did she say?"

The irascible woman had called to complain about Heather and Jenny. She warned Betty Sue to keep them away from her house.

"She called you a wolf in sheep's clothing. Accused you of being there to plant evidence against her."

"But why would I do that?" Jenny cried.

Heather declared the woman was going on the offensive to intimidate them.

"What that means is that she has something to hide."

Star was looking worried.

"Didn't you say she is prone to violence? I think you should stay away from her, sweetie." She clutched Jenny's hand for support. "The woman sounds mad to me."

Molly thought she was cunning. Phyllis was a frequent visitor to the library and often went to great lengths to acquire any book she wanted.

"She only reads books about gardening, of course. Wants us to order every new one that is released. If the book she wants is checked out, she lurks in the library and pressures us into showing her who has it. I've heard she goes after them."

Heather was grinning from ear to ear, clearly enjoying this bizarre account of a woman she didn't like.

"This is all just hearsay," Molly began. "She hounds them around town – at the grocery store or post office, for example. Or she calls them, begging them to return the book."

Betty Sue was astounded. How had she never heard about these things?

"Phyllis is looking more and more guilty now," Jenny sighed. "You should have seen the hatred in her eyes when she spoke about Paddy."

But what did the police think, the others wanted to know.

Jenny told them how Shirley was top on their list of suspects.

"But I'm sure she will turn out to be innocent. We don't know much about their dynamics, of course. They seemed happy though."

Heather agreed with her.

"Paddy had his arm around her at the town meeting. He cared a lot about her. And have you noticed what a fashion plate she is? Wearing those pricey shoes? I'm sure he loved spending money on her."

Had Shirley been with Paddy for his money then?

"She's the kind of arm candy older men desire. We can presume they both got what they wanted from each other."

Phyllis Tross had not pointed a finger at Shirley which was strange. If the woman wanted to divert suspicion from herself, wouldn't she use someone else as a stooge?

"Oh yes! She told us a man had been spying on Paddy."

Heather reiterated her opinion. There was no such man. Phyllis had used him to distract them.

"Is it possible she is really sick?" Molly mused. "I mean, what if she's seeing strange men where there are none? Just like she is accusing Paddy of stealing her flowers. She genuinely believes it or she would not have said so in front of the whole town."

Star's frown deepened. Jenny felt her tension mount.

"I don't think Phyllis is mentally ill. She has complete control over her emotions and actions."

Either way, the woman could not be taken lightly, Star warned.

"You won't go to her house alone, for any reason. Promise me, Jenny."

"Okay, okay. I'll do whatever you say." Jenny patted her shoulder, reassuring her.

Phyllis and Shirley were the only options then, Heather summed up. The police would not need long to wrap up this case.

Molly shook her head. Weren't they forgetting something?

"Paddy was found in a stranger's house."

Jenny told them what she knew about the owner. He lived in the city and had only come there to fix the heater. The police would verify his story.

"But what about the man who was renting that house?" Molly shot back. "I think he's a part of this puzzle."

Chapter 11

Molly returned to the library. Heather and Betty Sue stayed on.

"Ada is coming here, Jenny. I don't think she'll stay for lunch though. Too rustic for the likes of her."

Jenny was well aware of Ada Newbury's preference for the country club. She liked to remind everyone that she was the richest woman in town. The Newburys were rumored to have a stash of gold that came from buried treasure. It was one of the legends Jenny had been in awe with when she first came to Pelican Cove.

"I don't mind, Betty Sue. Are you two having a secret meeting?"

Apart from Barb Norton, who was currently spending winter with her daughter in Florida, Ada Newbury was an active participant in town matters. She didn't lower herself to do menial work but liked to throw her weight around. Mostly, she reminded everyone that she was an important stakeholder since it was her money that funded most of the town events.

"Ada wants to discuss the winter festival. But she's late."

Jenny felt the hair on her neck stand up. Footsteps sounded in the distance. Ada swept in, swathed in black from head to toe with a silk pashmina over her shoulder.

"Hello Betty Sue."

"You were supposed to be here thirty minutes ago," Betty Sue grumbled. "My time is more valuable than yours."

Ada barely glanced at Jenny and ignored the others, looking around, searching for something.

"Pull up a chair and sit." Betty Sue growled. "Not good enough for you?"

Ada obeyed but sat down gingerly, close to the edge.

"Why didn't you agree to meet at the country club? They have lobster mac and cheese today and I'm going to miss it because of you."

Jenny sat at an adjoining table, trying not to laugh. The two adversaries were well matched and did their best to outdo each other every time they met.

"Holding a winter festival is out of question. It will take too many resources."

The two ladies agreed for once.

"I'm surprised you are being so sensible," Betty Sue replied. "Should we wait to count the ballots?"

Ada made a dismissive motion with her hand. They would let the people vote. It made them feel important.

"We can offer a compromise. Just one dinner instead of a whole festival." She turned to stare at Jenny. "You can hold it here."

"I am sorry. We are going to be closed for renovation." Jenny was quick to respond. "Do you mean dinner for the whole town? That sounds equally daunting."

A light drizzle had started again and Heather had been watching the rain, looking like she was least interested in what was happening around her. But Jenny knew she was listening to every word.

"Do you think Pelican Cove needs a new restaurant?"

Ada ignored her but Jenny saw a blush creep up her face.

"Not fancy enough for the country club set?" Heather needled.

Ada opened her mouth to say something but clammed up.

"Don't interrupt, Heather."

Betty Sue may be pushing ninety but she was sharp as a tack. Jenny cheered silently when she confronted Ada.

"What do you know about this business, Ada? I can tell when you're holding back."

With a shrug, Ada turned to Jenny.

"Are you playing detective again, Jenny? I heard they found a dead body on the island."

"A friend wants me to look into it," Jenny admitted, without revealing Shirley's name.

She was sure the two women would not be acquainted.

"I pity your husband," Ada clucked. "You should've settled down by now, appreciated what a gem Jason is. Instead, you choose to play cat and mouse with the Sheriff."

Heather surged to Jenny's defence.

"Adam respects her opinion. Jenny's almost like a consultant for the police now."

A few customers came in and Jenny got up to serve them. Heather joined her and began assembling sandwiches. They hardly noticed the time until Star came in.

"Betty Sue's in a tizzy. It's past her lunch hour."

Jenny glanced at the clock and realized it was after one in the afternoon. She ladled soup and plated the sandwiches. Star had already found a tray.

"I can handle it from here. Will you join us?"

The last customer was just leaving. Jenny nodded and urged Heather to go ahead.

"I'm right behind ya."

She loaded another tray and walked out on the deck, surprised to see Ada Newbury hadn't left.

"Are you sure I can't get you anything?" She winced. "I can rustle up a quick salad if you want."

Ada gave a slight shudder and shook her head.

"I'll be on my way soon. But thanks!"

With a slight smirk, she offered to help Jenny in her investigation.

"Maybe you can take that uppity sheriff down a notch."

Jenny was perplexed by this unexpected gesture. She dug her spoon in her soup and took a sip, waiting for the imperious woman to continue.

"Julius, my husband, took me to dinner a few days ago. It was our anniversary."

"To the country club?" Heather quipped.

"No, Heather," Ada bristled. "It was a special night. So he took me to Onancock for a romantic dinner."

Jenny couldn't predict where she was going with the story but she forced herself to be patient, taking a bite of her chicken sandwich.

"Julius is such a dear. One of his friends recommended this place. It's tucked away on a private beach and is run by a Michelin star chef." She turned to Heather when she said that. "That means ..."

"I know what a Michelin star is," Heather cut her off.

"Okay," Ada laughed. "So you know such places are not cheap. And the wine! Let's say a meal for two costs four figures."

Betty Sue muttered under her breath. Jenny heard something about waste and chuckled.

"Is there a point to all this?" Betty Sue barked. "Or are you just showing off how you squander your ill gotten gains?"

Ignoring her outburst, Ada stared at Jenny.

"Who do you think I saw there, having dinner with a man who was not her husband?" She gave a dramatic pause. "That woman Shirley! Paddy's wife."

Jenny's eyebrows shot up. Ada had finally managed to get everyone's attention. But she was wrong about one thing.

"Shirley was not Paddy's wife. They weren't actually married."

Ada thought it was just a technicality. The point was, Shirley was at a rendezvous with another man. It was clearly an assignation of sorts, given how the couple was huddled together, engrossed in their conversation.

"This is a strong motive, isn't it? Shirley killed Paddy because she wanted to be with this other man. And one more thing. He seemed a bit humble, compared to Paddy."

"You mean poor!" Heather snorted.

Ada didn't reprimand her this time. The man wore faded chinos and a shirt with a frayed collar.

Jenny pointed out that Shirley could have walked out on Paddy any time. In her mind, she was wondering if this man was the reason Shirley was going to leave town.

"I think Shirley was planning to run with this man. But she needed Paddy's money. So the two of them killed him."

Betty Sue played Devil's Advocate, suggesting Shirley might be meeting the man for any reason. Maybe she wanted to surprise Paddy and this guy was helping her get a unique present.

Ada flashed them a look of triumph.

"That is why I saved the best for last. I liked the restaurant so much, I begged Julius to take me there again."

They had gone to the same restaurant three days later. Shirley was there too, with the same man.

"They looked pretty cozy, if you know what I mean."

Jenny couldn't hold back her excitement.

"Thank you for telling me all this, Ms. Ada. Shirley was so upset by Paddy's death, I was reluctant to believe her guilt. But this gives her a strong motive."

Ada left after that, a smile of triumph making her look more odious than usual.

"Well?" Jenny faced Betty Sue. "Do you think she was fibbing?"

Ada Newbury did not tell white lies, Betty Sue replied, almost reluctantly. And she lacked the imagination to make up a story like that.

They were silent as they finished lunch. Jenny was all talked out. She just wanted to go home and lounge before the television.

Heather accompanied Betty Sue home. Star was meeting Jimmy. Jenny had the kitchen to herself. She tidied up, trying to come up with ideas about how she would serve her regulars when the kitchen was out of commission.

"Knock, knock." A gruff voice called. "Can a man get a spot of lunch around here?"

"Adam!" Jenny greeted. "You almost missed me."

He apologized for being late and guessed Jenny had run out of food.

"Why don't we grab something at Ethan's? We can talk on the way. If you can spare the time, that is."

Jenny opened the fridge and took an inventory. She could rustle up a quick meal easily.

"No, no. Sit. I can make an omelet if that's okay."

Adam settled at the kitchen counter and munched on a stick of celery. Jenny beat eggs, rendered some sausage in the pan and poured the eggs in. She added a handful of sharp cheddar before folding the omelet.

"Toast?" she offered.

Adam thought a moment, then shook his head.

"I'd rather have one of those cookies later."

Jenny waited until he took a few bites before launching into her questions.

"So? Do you have any updates?" She could barely wait to give him her scoop.

"I see you are bursting to tell me something. Why don't you go first?"

Jenny narrated Ada's story, watching his face for any reaction.

"You don't seem impressed."

"Ada Newbury maybe the richest woman in town, but she leads a predictable life. I think she's hankering for some attention."

Jenny told him she had thought the same. But Betty Sue was sure Ada wasn't lying. Jenny had thought Adam would be thrilled to be able to pin a motive on Shirley.

"Wasn't Shirley your main suspect? You said as much last night."

Adam wanted an iron clad case. That would require solid evidence.

"Did Ada remember anything about this man?"

"She said he was poor." Jenny blurted.

Adam guffawed when he heard that, spearing the last bit of omelet with his fork.

"Ada thinks every person in town is poor compared to her." He reflected on his words. "Which is true in a way, I guess."

Unwilling to back down, Jenny told him there was more. She tried to remember every detail Ada had mentioned and passed it on to him.

"And yes, he drives a beat up old Chevy. Oh, and wait! Ada surmised he might walk with a limp or have some kind of disability. She saw a cane propped up by his table."

Adam had been giving her his full attention. His eyes widened at the mention of the Chevy. When Jenny mentioned the cane, his face broke into a knowing smile.

"That sounds like Hank Smith. He's the new science teacher at the high school." He picked up a cookie from the plate before him. "Has a degree from some big university in the Midwest and several trophies. Jenny, he's harmless."

She wasn't ready to give up that easily.

"Okay, but why is he so far away from home? And what was he up to, having a romantic dinner with Shirley?"

Chapter 12

Jenny was exhausted when she got home. It had been a strange day. She wanted to forget everything about the murder and let her hair down. A night out with friends seemed like a good idea.

She suggested going out for drinks when Jason came home. He was all for it.

"I'm craving something crunchy and greasy. Let's go to the Crab Shack."

Jenny's mouth watered at the thought of the crispy onion rings Ethan's was famous for. She gave in readily and called the Bayview Inn.

"Coming to the Crab Shack?" she asked Heather.

Betty Sue opted to stay home. Jenny guessed Star would visit with her. She turned out to be right.

"Do you want to go to Ethan's with us?" she asked when her aunt sauntered in, looking pleased. "Betty Sue's staying in."

"Then I'll keep her company. You don't mind, sweetie?"

Jenny assured her she was fine with it. Heather was going to call Molly.

"What about Billy?" Jenny thought out loud.

"I thought you wanted to destress," Jason teased. "Let's give Billy a rain check."

Jenny laughed at his attempt at humor.

"When do you want to leave?"

There was an hour or more of daylight left.

"It's barely four, sweetheart. Why don't we leave after six? I have to do some research on a case."

Jenny asked if she could go out for a walk, sure of Jason's answer. She dressed in a pair of jeans and pulled on her favorite cable knit sweater. The clouds had receded a bit and there was no sign of rain. It was still chilly outside.

She stepped out of the house and got into her car, waving her hand when Jason came to the window. She had prevaricated a bit. The walk she had mentioned was going to be on the boardwalk.

Jenny pulled up outside the Bayview Inn and honked. Heather came out, curious.

"You are coming with me."

Jenny took her arm and led her to the Boardwalk.

"Did you forget something at the café?"

They came across a group of cheerleaders, practising their routine. Jenny tipped her head at the girls and asked Heather if she knew any of them.

"Not exactly the age group I hang out with." Heather taunted.

Jenny ignored the jibe and waited for a valid response.

"I think I recognize one or two ... that tow headed, curly one looks familiar. No wait, she looks like one of the characters in a cartoon I'm watching."

"Anything else?"

Heather took a few steps toward the girls and narrowed her eyes.

"That short one with the freckles ... she's the exact image of a girl I went to school with. We were lab partners in our senior year."

Jenny told her she was going to ask after her long lost friend. They went closer to the group and watched them for a while. A girl who was obviously their leader called for a break after some time. She came to talk to them.

"How are you, Ms. Jenny?"

"Very well, thank you. You've shot up, haven't you, Amy?" Jenny realized the girl came to the café with her mom for pancakes.

The girl with freckles joined them.

"Are you Toni's kid?" Heather asked. "Your mom and I were in the same class. We won a prize at the science fair once."

The girl bobbed her head and gave a wide smile, showing off a set of dimples.

"She told me about that. I'm doing a project for the fair this year, see? Amy's my partner."

Jenny couldn't believe her luck.

"You can ask Heather to guide you."

"No way!" Heather cracked up. "It's been an age since I was in school. Don't you have a good teacher?"

Amy said they had the best possible one.

"Old Mr. Woods retired last year. Mr. Smith teaches us now and he's very smart."

"Handsome too," the other girl gushed.

The two collapsed in a fit of giggles.

Heather wanted to know more about this man. Was he local? Amy volunteered he had moved to Pelican Cove recently.

"He lived in some place near Chicago. That's in the Midwest. They have snow!"

"Lots of it," Toni's daughter added.

Jenny remarked they knew a lot about him. He sounded very friendly.

"Is he married?" Heather probed. "Maybe I'll ask him on a date."

The girls laughed wildly. Amy told her that wasn't possible because he had a girlfriend. They had seen him with her multiple times.

Heather's attempt to find out more about the woman did not yield much.

Amy glanced at her watch and blew on a whistle. Their break was over and they had to get back to rehearsing their formations.

"See ya soon, Ms. Jenny!" Amy beamed.

"Pancakes on the house next time," Jenny promised.

Heather fell in step with her and they walked back to the inn.

"I guess you know this guy Smith they were talking about?"

Jenny brought her up to speed on what Adam had said. Although the girls hadn't taken any names, she was almost sure the girlfriend they had seen with their teacher was Shirley.

"Hank Smith. New teacher at the Pelican Cove High School. Poor but smart and handsome. Do you still want to date him?"

Heather gave her a mock push.

"I was just trying to speak their language."

"And you did good!"

That brought a rare smile.

"My stomach's growling, Jenny. I think it's time to head to the Shack."

They rode back to Seaview to get Jason.

"Nice walk?" he asked with a grin.

"The best!" Jenny replied.

Molly was going to meet them at the Shack. She sat at a table beside the water, chatting with Billy.

"Oh, oh." Jenny stole a glance at Heather. "I swear I didn't invite him."

"I did."

She went forward and greeted him with a hug.

"Have you ordered yet? I'm ready to eat."

Ethan materialized, accompanied by two servers. One of them carried drinks while the other held a tray loaded with a variety of appetizers.

"Onion rings and mozzarella sticks," Jenny drooled, accepting a glass of sangria. "I've been dreaming about these, Ethan!"

He told them to eat up.

As if by a silent accord, they stuck to safe topics like movies and music. Heather acted as if she had never had any problem with Billy. After some initial hesitation, he assumed his formal persona and made small talk.

They ate beer battered fried fish and coconut shrimp, followed by warm bread pudding for dessert. It had ribbons of blackberry compote in it and Ethan served it with cinnamon ice cream.

"This is nice!" Billy yawned. "We should come here again when Nick's in town, Jenny."

Heather's eyes flickered. Did she have a problem with Nick, Jenny wondered. They would be at an impasse if that was so. Billy loved his son and no matter how much he loved Heather, he would always want Nick to be a big part of their life.

Jason settled the bill and the group got up to leave. Ethan came along to say goodbye.

"The food was delicious," Jenny complimented. "Why do I never see you at the Boardwalk Café?"

"I keep long hours," he smiled. "You know how it is in the food business. Say Jenny, what's this I hear about you redecorating?"

She told him he had heard right. It was high time the café got a face lift.

"Molly and I are working on some ideas. Maybe we can sound them off you."

Ethan was very enthusiastic and they made plans to meet one afternoon.

Jenny was warm and content as she walked out of the shack, arm in arm with Heather and Molly. The island had given her new life. She had the love of a good man, staunch friends and a passion she could pursue every day. The future had a rosy outlook and she was thankful.

Heather was talking over her head with Molly, telling her about the cheerleaders. Jason and Billy were debating going for a game of golf at the club. Jenny was trying to follow both conversations at once.

She reached her car and walked to the passenger side, since Jason was their designated driver. So she didn't notice the paper tucked under the wiper blades at first.

"What's that?" Heather pointed.

Jenny leaned across the hood and tugged, afraid she might tear the paper. There were no cops going around handing parking tickets in Pelican Cove. If anyone wanted to give her a message, they could have come inside and talked to her.

She unfolded the piece of paper and stared, unable to focus for a split second. A gasp escaped and she began to tremble.

"Gimme that!" Heather snatched the paper from her hands.

Jason's arm came around Jenny and held her tight. His face had turned grim. They all waited for Heather to say something.

"It's a threat."

She handed the paper to Billy.

"Egads!" His relaxed manner had been replaced by rapid breathing. "Some idiot's drawn a cupcake with a knife stuck in it. The message warns Jenny to mind her own business and let the police do their job."

Jenny found her cheeks were wet. This was not the first time she had faced danger while solving a murder. Her mind rushed ahead, trying to ascertain who might have written the note.

"At least she's giving me a warning." Her attempt at humor fell flat.

Jason ushered her into the car, eager to reach the safety of their house.

"Can you see Heather gets home safely?" he asked Billy.

For once, Heather didn't protest or make any claims about not needing a man's help. She told Jason to keep an eye out for trouble.

Jenny was quiet on the drive back home, barely holding it together. She would not let a random note spoil their mood.

"Dinner was great, wasn't it?"

Jason's lips were set in a line. He kept glancing into the rearview mirror.

"Billy's escorting us home."

Jenny wasn't surprised. Despite their turbulent past, she was the mother of his child and he cared for her wellbeing. They pulled up outside Seaview. Star was pacing in the driveway. She rushed forward and came to Jenny's side.

"Molly called. She's notified Adam."

Jenny thought they were making a fuss for nothing.

"Phyllis is being dramatic."

Billy flashed his lights and made a three point turn, giving them a wave. Jenny waved back. Star offered hot chocolate when they went inside.

"Good idea!" Jason thanked her. "Add a stiff shot of brandy in it."

There was a soft glow from the fire and the room was pleasantly warm. But Jason placed a blanket around Jenny's shoulders.

"I know it's futile, asking you to step back," he squirmed. "But will you at least promise to be careful?"

Star came out, bearing a tray of hot chocolate.

"One of us will be with her all the time. Don't you worry, Jason."

Jenny did not mind being coddled. Her aunt and husband were naturally worried about her safety. She had barely begun to look into Paddy's death and had not expected her efforts would rattle anyone.

"Poor Paddy!" she reminisced. "He offered to make the Boardwalk Café a household name." A small laugh escaped her. "Paddy said we could go national. And he would help us get the necessary funding. He told me I must dream big, Jase. A man I'd barely met once!"

He was the helpful sort then, Jason mused. Why would anyone kill him?

"He's a newcomer," Star informed them. "Barely eight, nine years since he came to live in Pelican Cove."

Jenny knew her aunt had been living there for over forty years but was still not considered a local.

"That's a long enough time to make enemies. Phyllis Tross is the only one who admits having a problem with him."

Star reminded her about the man who had been lurking outside Paddy's home.

"We know nothing about him, Jenny. It's time to find out more."

Chapter 13

Jenny slept soundly and woke five minutes before her alarm went off. But she was reluctant to get out of bed. Jason sat up and pulled her in his arms.

"Why don't you take the day off? Star and Heather can handle breakfast. Or we can stay closed today. It will be good practice for when you are closed for the renovation."

That spurred her into action.

"No, Jason. The poor dears are going to be inconvenienced later anyway. It's not right to add to their discomfort."

He stood his ground and asked if she was feeling up to it.

"At least let me come along. I can put on an apron and work beside you."

Jenny felt a rush of emotion, thinking she didn't deserve Jason.

"Don't you have to go to the city today? No, no. I'm not going to cower and hide in a dark corner, just because someone played a silly prank on me."

A hot shower improved her mood and she set off after pulling on her favorite outfit. She rubbed the charms around her neck as she rode to the café, thinking about her son.

Jenny switched on all the lights once she reached the café. The sky was overcast again. She had prepped a pan of French Toast the previous day. All she had to do was slide it in the oven. Feeling the need to stay busy, she set about making a sauce to go with it, using frozen berries.

Captain Charlie arrived right on time. He took one look at her face and demanded to know what was wrong.

"You've been brooding over something, missy. I can tell."

She poured out the story of the threatening note. Captain Charlie muttered a few curses under his breath, shaking his head from side to side.

"Beg your pardon, Jenny. But what has this town come to? Never thought a body would have to look over their shoulder in Pelican Cove. But you don't worry. There's plenty here who have your back."

Jenny went into the kitchen to fry some spicy sausages. Captain Charlie walked to the deck and sat down. She suspected he had changed his plans and was staying on to keep her company.

He dug into his French Toast like a man who had missed his dinner, praising it to the skies.

"Are there cloves in this sauce?" he licked the spoon, pulling out an ancient cellphone from his pocket. "You write down my number, Jenny. Call me whenever you need some muscle. These old bones still have a fight left in them."

She thanked him, reminding him she already had it.

"So you don't think I should give up looking into this murder?"

He paused, holding his fork midair. His eyes twinkled with mischief.

"Do you want to?"

Jenny shook her head. She would not let herself be frightened by anonymous threats. And she was certainly not going to be coerced by a cold blooded killer.

Captain Charlie asked for a second cup of coffee and lingered. She knew he would stick around and keep an eye on her. A few customers arrived and Jenny got busy serving them.

Star arrived just as the phone in the kitchen rang.

"Mom!" Nick's voice traveled over the wires, making her face light up in a broad smile. "You've landed in trouble again!"

"Then you better come down and be my bodyguard," she shot back.

Nick promised to be there over the weekend. He was buried under a mountain of work since he had just got back from a long vacation.

"I warned Dad he better make sure you're in one piece."

Jenny groaned. That meant Billy would hound every step she took.

"Everything's fine, Nicky. But I do miss you."

Star hovered over her shoulder, looking tense. She urged Jenny to take a break and eat something after she hung up.

"Why not sit and have a bite? This French Toast looks mighty appealing."

Jenny complied. She was drawing up a lunch menu, determined to keep herself busy by making something elaborate.

A generous helping of the sweet and spicy French Toast and a steaming cup of coffee gave her a new burst of energy. She trooped back to the kitchen and began peeling carrots.

"We are making roasted carrot hummus, kale salad and tuna melts," she announced. "Spread the word."

If Star thought it was ambitious, she didn't say so. The carrots were roasting in the oven, along with a few shallots and a bulb of garlic. Jenny was massaging the kale when the phone rang again.

"Can you please get that?" she called out to Star who was topping up a customer's coffee.

She ambled in and picked up the receiver, her eyebrows shooting up. Was it shock or surprise, Jenny couldn't say.

"Yes." Star paused. "Is that really necessary?" She twirled the cord around her fingers. "I'll give her the message but I can't promise anything."

Jenny's mind was throwing out all kinds of theories.

"Who was that?" she asked before Star could say a word.

"Wilson. From the garage. Has some urgent business with you, sweetie. But he wouldn't tell me more than that."

Was her car due for an oil change, Jenny wondered. Wilson wouldn't call that urgent, would he? Why was he being secretive?

"And you have no idea what he's going on about?"

"None."

Jenny set the bowl of salad aside and washed her hands at the sink. She would have to go to the garage. The lunch prep was under control and she had some free time.

"Why don't you take Heather with you?" Star suggested. "You did promise Jason you would take one of us with you when you ventured anywhere."

Jenny tamped down her frustration and nodded. Her aunt meant well. And it was too soon since the nasty note.

"You wishing me to perdition?" Heather breezed in and sampled a piece of kale.

Jenny laughed and told her about the impending trip.

"You are to be my body woman."

Heather agreed to accompany her without hesitation but insisted on eating first.

"I'm not missing that French Toast."

Jenny had set aside a plate for her. Heather plunged a fork in and smacked her lips when she tasted the sauce.

"So delicious! What about the flan?"

Jenny hadn't forgotten. She had already tried out a few batches at home and was ready to try some at the café.

"I'll make some for lunch today, if we get back in time."

Heather offered to drive. Jenny declined, trying to curb her annoyance.

"You don't have to treat me with kid gloves. I'm not such a ninnyhammer I can't manage to control my car."

With a shrug, Heather slid into the passenger seat and snapped on her seatbelt. The drive to the Wilson Auto Shop was not long. Jenny made a turn just after the bridge that led off the island came in sight.

A tall, dark haired man dressed in overalls came out, wiping his hands on a rag. He led them to his tiny office.

"What's on your mind, Peter?" Jenny questioned. "Have you called me in for an oil change?"

He snorted, swiveling from side to side in his chair.

"I woulda' sent a boy to pick up your car." His gaze hardened. "No, Ms. Jenny. I got some news for you."

Jenny's pulse quickened. Wilson came from an unusual background. Few people in town knew about his past, other than her and the police. He had led a blameless life for several years but he still had connections.

"Was Paddy one of you guys?"

His face stretched into a grin.

"The bloke who got himself stabbed in one of those new bungalows?"

Jenny nodded, waiting for him to go on.

"I lead a simple life now. And the garage keeps me busy."

Heather was getting restless.

"What are we doing here, Peter? Come to the point."

"I'm sure you must be hard on the killer's trail, Ms. Jenny. I know you well." He stopped swiveling and placed his elbows on the table, leaning closer to them. "I can tell you something that will knock your socks off."

The threatening note was uppermost in Jenny's mind.

"You know who placed that paper on my windshield?"

Wilson's eyes clouded. He had no idea what she was talking about.

"Jenny got a warning to stay away from the investigation," Heather supplied. "Are you going to tell us who it was?"

Peter sighed and shook his head. He wasn't aware of any notes.

"Sounds like I gotta keep an eye on you. Ms. Petunia would've wanted that."

Jenny assured him she was fine and able to take care of herself. If he didn't know about the note, why had he summoned them to the garage? He dropped a bombshell she hadn't seen coming.

Peter and his wife attended all the town meetings, just like any good citizen of Pelican Cove. He had been present when Phyllis Tross leveled her allegations against Paddy, calling him a thief. She had been sitting in a row behind them and he heard her spewing all kinds of threats. The venom in her voice would have shaken the coolest man.

"She has no hold over her temper, that one." Peter grinned. "I have it on good authority the woman's resorted to violence more than once in her life."

Jenny agreed with him. She admitted having her suspicions about Phyllis. The woman appeared unhinged but there was no evidence that she had actually done something to hurt Paddy.

"That's where I come in," Wilson beamed. "I can place her at the scene of the crime."

Jenny was flabbergasted. Did that also mean Wilson had seen her stab him?

"What were you doing at that bungalow?"

"Not me." Peter was patient. "Mrs. Tross. She brought her car in for servicing. I have heard the rumors flying around town, of course. And I know that man was her sworn enemy."

Jenny wished he would hurry up. She forced herself to be patient, not wanting to interrupt.

Wilson had carried out his regular checks on the vehicle. He had then looked at the inbuilt tracking device and struck gold.

According to the data in the instrument, Phyllis had been at the address where the body was found.

"On the same morning. I can give you the exact time."

Jenny didn't ask if he had reported this to the police. Peter Wilson would never approach them on his own, not unless absolutely necessary.

"This is tremendous!" Jenny exclaimed. "Thank you for telling me, Peter."

He shrugged and spread his arms wide, his mouth settling in a smug smile.

"I figured I'd help you a bit, Ms. Jenny. But why don't you sit this one out, huh? You barely knew that man."

He was an innocent victim and that was enough, Jenny replied. She thanked Wilson again and came out of the garage, feeling exhilarated.

"Phyllis Tross has a motive and we can place her at that house," she summed up on the drive back to the café. "She's the top suspect as of now."

Heather agreed that Wilson coming through was a stroke of luck.

"I never liked that Shirley. But I also have first hand experience of how cruel Phyllis Tross can be."

They still hadn't proven anything, Jenny reminded her.

"I believe Shirley's a gold digger and had a good time on Paddy's money. But ..."

Heather finished her line of thought.

"Why would she kill the golden goose?"

Chapter 14

Jenny buzzed with excitement as she prepared lunch. The latest information she had received meant they were very close. Phyllis Tross would be taken in for questioning. She wondered what explanation she would provide for being in the vicinity of the crime. Was the woman wily enough to have prepared a plausible story?

The carrots were perfectly roasted, tender and smoky with a slight char on them. Jenny added all the ingredients to the food processor and thought of Shirley. She was free to do what she wanted now. Did that involve a future with the new school teacher? Jenny transferred the hummus to a bowl and scooped a tiny bit with a spoon. Was there too much garlic?

Star came in, wanting to know about her visit to the garage. Jenny supplied a brief overview.

"Do you think this has too much garlic?"

Star tasted the hummus and shook her head. It would be masked by the bread and other veggies Jenny added to the sandwich.

Betty Sue and Molly had arrived in their absence. They were on their way out but they were also eager to get the latest scoop. Jenny glanced at the clock and panicked. The lunch guests would begin to arrive soon.

She hurried out to the deck to talk to her friends.

"How about a spa session tonight? It's been a while."

They all agreed, even Heather, who had been nibbling on a cookie with a lost look on her face.

"Don't bring brownies," Jenny told Molly, eliciting a groan from the others. "I'll make flan. It's time we started testing my recipe."

News of the slightly different lunch menu had already spread in town. Jenny was surprised to see Captain Charlie. Had he stuck around just so he could keep an eye on her?

"What have you been up to?" she gave him a mock glare, placing a tuna melt before him. "Nothing good, I'm sure."

He gave a mischievous grin but was quite evasive, deflecting attention by praising the sandwich.

"This has just the right amount of Old Bay, which is plenty."

Jenny flushed with pleasure and admitted she could hardly eat anything without the favorite local spice. She chatted with him as she served the customers, noticing he hung around until the café was empty.

Star was perusing some designs Molly had brought along. Jenny was eager to take a look. She had just fixed a plate for them when Adam sauntered in, looking peeved.

"Am I too late?"

Jenny hoped his irritation stemmed from hunger. She knew Adam hated tuna melts.

"How about carrot hummus?" she quizzed. "And there's some kale salad."

Adam told her that would be great. Jenny added extra cucumbers and tomatoes to his sandwich, along with a generous handful of feta cheese. She cut it in two and put it on a plate, taking it out to the deck. Star was telling Adam about the room that would be dedicated to her art.

"This is a brilliant idea, Jenny. I'm sure sales will skyrocket."

Star was anxious she would not be able to keep up with the demand.

They ate with relish, Jenny surprised she found the hummus tastier than the tuna melt. She would add it to the summer menu.

"Are you revamping the menu too?" It was as if Adam read her thoughts. "I hope you keep the old classics like chicken salad."

Jenny assured him she wouldn't do anything drastic.

"Not with the café," Adam nodded, narrowing his eyes. "Never with the café. But when it comes to your own person, Jenny, you are willing to take any risk."

Here it comes, Jenny thought, watching Adam dab his mouth with a paper napkin. He had come to chastise her.

"What have I done now?" She tried to sound merry.

Adam's mouth drooped. He wasn't going to blame her for someone else's actions.

"You are the victim here. I'm sorry you don't trust me enough to come to me."

Jenny asked what he was talking about. Was this about that silly note?

"I've been thinking. It must be a prank. You know how boring the winter term is. It stretches on and on before you with no end in sight. I suspect a bunch of high school kids were having some fun."

"Really?" Adam was skeptical. "I don't mean to alarm you but we should take it seriously."

Did she have the note? He wanted to have it analyzed.

Jenny nodded. She had tucked it in her bag that morning, just in case.

"Billy has a big mouth. I warned him not to blab to you."

Adam told her Billy had been the last one to call him.

"Captain Charlie was waiting for me at the station. Then Jason came in, followed by Heather. Then Betty Sue telephoned and threatened all kinds of dire punishments if I didn't do something about it."

He began to tap his fingers on the table, pinning her with a glare.

"You promised you would not keep me in the dark, Jenny. About anything. How am I going to protect you if you hide such vital information from me?"

Jenny held up her hands, accepting defeat.

"I'm sorry. I apologize, okay. It doesn't feel good, being fussed over. Sometimes I feel I'm taking undue advantage of the people who love me."

Star did not mince words, ordering her to stop acting like a stranger.

Adam took the note and put it in a plastic bag, lamenting over how many people had already handled it.

"This is it? You are not keeping anything else from me?"

Star began piling the empty plates on a tray and beat a hasty retreat.

Jenny informed Adam about her trip to the Wilson Auto Shop.

"What does the autopsy report say? When did the crime happen?"

It was in the morning hours, Adam replied. His ears turned red as he heard about the data Wilson had read off the tracking device.

"He should have reported this to the police! I can arrest him for withholding vital information."

Jenny told him to calm down.

"Don't be silly. You know Peter Wilson doesn't trust the police. Given his background, he's bound to keep his distance."

What if they had never found this out, Adam quizzed. Jenny wished he would focus on what Wilson's information had made possible. He could question Phyllis Tross.

With a sigh, Adam agreed she was right.

"I'm glad he did talk to you. You were right, Jenny. People open up to you. They trust you will be kind to them, I suppose, unlike the police."

Jenny lifted a shoulder in a shrug.

"You're doing your job, Adam. And that's necessary too. Can we just agree we make a good team?"

He gave her a lopsided smile.

"Since we are swapping information, let me tell you what else has come to light."

Jenny sat forward in her chair, all agog. Adam's words shocked her.

"We found a partial finger print on the murder weapon. It's clear that someone wiped the surfaces in the house, hoping to remove any evidence but they missed a spot."

"That's good, right?"

"Can you guess who they belong to?"

"Phyllis?" Jenny's eyes widened.

That would prove the woman's guilt without any doubt.

"Shirley Brown."

"What?" Jenny cried. "Are you sure?"

With a snort, Adam told her he was positive. The evidence could not be denied. It meant Shirley was certainly a suspect.

"It not only puts her in the vicinity, it proves she was right there in that house with Paddy. And it was probably her hand that wielded the knife."

Jenny's thoughts flew to Hank Smith. Why was Adam overlooking his connection to Shirley?

"You have plenty to think about then," she smiled.

Adam nodded, stating it was high time he went back to the station.

"Thank you for the lunch, Jenny. And keep an eye out for anything unusual."

Jenny promised to be careful. She was sure there would be someone with her wherever she went.

Star drove home with her, proving her right.

"What are your plans now, sweetie?"

"A nap, a bath and then I'm going to be in the kitchen, making flan. Why don't you go and meet Jimmy?"

Star blushed and told her he was on his way over. He would leave before the Magnolias arrived for spa night.

Resigned to being cosseted, Jenny scampered up the stairs and flopped on her bed. The sun was low in the sky when she opened her eyes and sat up. She ran a bath and sat in the window, watching the sunset while the tub filled. A few drops of lavender oil would set the mood for a relaxing evening.

She dressed in a pair of old flannel pajamas, pulling on a comfy robe. A buzz of voices traveled up the stairs. It looked like Betty Sue and Heather had arrived. Eager to join them, she hurried downstairs.

"Hello ladies!" she collapsed at one end of the couch and slapped her forehead with her hand. "I forgot the flan!"

Betty Sue and Star sat in their favorite overstuffed chairs, their feet already soaking in buckets of warm water.

Heather looked up from filing her nails.

"Oh no, Jenny! So we have no dessert?"

Jenny apologized and offered to call Jason. He could pick something up on his way home.

"No need!" Molly came in, holding a large Tupperware container they were familiar with. "I brought brownies, just in case." She blushed a bit. "Don't think I meant to undermine you, Jenny. But you can never have too much dessert, right? And I didn't want to come empty handed."

Jenny told her to calm down. She knew Molly had the best intentions.

"You are our savior, as it turns out. I slept so long and tarried in the bath. The flan just blew right out of my mind."

They got busy buffing nails, clipping cuticles and bickering over which shade of nail polish was the best. Star had set out some crackers with a bowl of pimento cheese. Jenny chomped on a few, then stopped. She didn't want to spoil her appetite. The doorbell chimed just then, heralding the arrival of their food.

"Who ordered the pizza?" she asked on her way to the door.

A pasty high school kid handed her the boxes and turned red as he thanked her for the generous tip.

They indulged in a slice or two of the steaming hot pies before Betty Sue broached the subject of the investigation.

"So it's a toss between Phyllis and Shirley."

Jenny wasn't surprised her friend was already aware of the latest development regarding Shirley Brown.

"No need to guess why Phyllis hated Paddy," Molly reasoned. "But what did Shirley have against him?"

"Too old," Heather quipped. "She spotted fresh meat and went after it."

With a pang, Jenny wondered if that was the reason Heather had distanced herself from Billy. Had she suddenly thought their age difference was too much?

Betty Sue rebuked her for being crude.

"Do you ever think before you speak? Sometimes I wonder where I went wrong in raising you."

That silenced Heather. Jenny saw her eyes flood with unshed tears and hastened to change the subject.

"Let's not forget that man who was spying on Paddy. We know nothing about him."

Betty Sue and Star both believed there was no such man. It was a ploy Phyllis Tross was using to distract Jenny and the police.

"Who will you talk to first?" Molly asked Jenny. "Shirley or this new man in her life?"

Savoring her last bite of pizza, Jenny took her time to answer.

"I think I am going to introduce myself to Hank Smith. Best catch him unawares."

Heather thought they might be too late. If Shirley was in cahoots with him, they would already prepare their answers and have them down pat.

Chapter 15

Spa night ended on a high note. Jason arrived when they were eating the brownies. He joined them for a while as they argued over which movie to watch. Choosing a sappy romantic comedy was a tradition they all enjoyed. It was a sure fire way to dispatch any unwanted men.

"I'm calling it a night," Jason yawned as soon as the credits rolled on the screen.

Although it was almost midnight when Jenny turned in, she slept soundly and woke up fresh, ready to tackle the day. Adam's question about a revamped menu had stuck with her and she was eager to try some new recipes.

The skies were clear on her drive to the café. A sunny day was expected and that would mean more people venturing out. Jenny made an extra pan of muffins for breakfast and shredded some gouda cheese, thinking of the best way to run into the school teacher. It had to seem natural, at least initially. She had no idea what kind of man he was. Better meet him at a public place.

Captain Charlie arrived right on time. He had never heard about Hank Smith.

"Don't go alone, Jenny."

She handed him his coffee and muffins, saying nothing. Was this going to be a problem? Heather would insist on going with her. Hank Smith would spot them a mile away and be on his guard.

Star was engrossed in finishing a custom painting. She called and told Jenny she would be late.

"Will you be okay, sweetie? Heather should be there soon."

Jenny was already beginning to suffocate under all this coddling. But she was grateful she had such people in her life.

Heather walked in when she had just finished mixing the chicken salad.

"Try this." She scooped some on a cracker and handed it to her.

Heather took a bite and closed her eyes, taking her task seriously.

"Wow! Do I taste lemon? And something herby. Basil, I think."

Jenny put some on another cracker and tasted it herself. It was very different from usual.

"Do you like it?"

"It's unexpected, since I'm so used to the usual taste. But it's refreshing. I do like it."

Heather was not sure what the locals would feel but tourists would love it.

"Most of the islanders are stick in the mud types. They just don't like change."

Jenny was going to make sandwiches with it for lunch. She was sure any reactions would be spontaneous.

She started a pot of soup while discussing the question that plagued her.

"How do I run into Hank Smith in a public place and also make it feel natural?"

Heather surprised her.

"Brown bag it. It's a beautiful day. This guy is from the Midwest, isn't he? My guess is he'll want to get some sun after being cooped up in a classroom all day."

She went ahead and packed a sandwich in a brown bag, along with some chips. Jenny added some cookies to another. The man could be innocent and a good person. She did not like going empty handed.

They had coffee after the Magnolias arrived. The ladies thought the plan had merit but it was hit or miss. What if Hank Smith did not come out to have lunch in the playground?

"Then you'll have a nice break from your own drudgery," Molly replied.

Star and Heather would manage the café while she was gone. Jenny begged them to let her go alone. One strange woman would garner less attention.

"And he has a preference for older women," Heather winked.

Jenny went in and tidied up, making sure she looked presentable. She grabbed the brown paper bags off the counter and set off toward the high school, fingers crossed.

She did not have a picture of Hank Smith but she looked around for someone matching Ada's description. Kids roamed outside the school. Many of them sat on benches, eating their lunch. There was a tiny bit of lawn beside the school, not really a park. But there was a large tree with a bench under it.

A hunched figure appeared, holding a lunch bag in one hand and a stick in another. The man walked with a slight limp and wore khakis and a blue button down shirt with a sweater vest. Assuming this was her quarry, Jenny picked up her step. She came to a halt a few paces before reaching him and looked around, as if trying to spot a bench.

"Hello!" she winced. "Do you mind if I sit here? A girl at the office told me about this park. But she failed to mention it had only one bench."

The man was perched at one end, and had just pulled out what looked like a peanut butter sandwich from his lunch bag.

He gave her a shrug and scooted a few inches more toward the corner.

Jenny left some space in between and sat down, placing her brown paper bag in the center. The man stared straight ahead and ate his sandwich in big bites. He would flee any minute.

Jenny pulled out her own sandwich and spoke again.

"Are you new? Haven't seen you around before."

He nodded. After a moment of hesitation, he slumped his shoulders in defeat.

"I am the new science teacher at the school." He tipped his head in the direction. "Hank Smith."

Jenny introduced herself.

"Do you live alone?" Jenny pointed at the sandwich. "That looks like something a man on his own would rustle up."

That drew a laugh from him.

"You caught me."

"Why don't you have this?" Jenny offered him her chicken sandwich. "I have more. Actually, I run a café and am trying out a new recipe. You'll be helping me by providing some valuable feedback."

As expected, he took her up on the offer. His eyebrows shot up after he swallowed a bite.

"That's delicious! I need to come to this café."

He admitted he hadn't been able to explore the town much. School started in the morning and he stayed back after it ended, catching up on admin tasks.

"I'm still getting to know the students. And I'm also organizing the science fair."

Jenny ate her own sandwich, taking in the view around her. A cold breeze ruffled her hair, making her shiver. She remarked on Hank's lack of coat.

"Aren't you cold?"

He laughed, his brown eyes shining with mirth. There were plenty of tiny lines around his eyes and mouth. Jenny gathered this was a person who was used to laughing a lot. She could almost see the allure Shirley must feel for him.

"I'm from the Midwest. We are used to harsher weather."

He was actually a bit warm in his sweater.

Jenny opened the packet of cookies and offered them to him. He took one readily.

"I have a horrible sweet tooth. And since I'm doing you a service ..."

They both chuckled at that.

"I would've invited you to the café but it's better you wait some time. Come after the renovation. Shirley must've mentioned that. Her designs are deceptively simple. But they are just what I'm looking for."

Hank went for a second cookie.

"Is this Shirley a friend of yours?"

So it was like that. Jenny had expected Hank would not own up to going out with Shirley, since they were meeting in secret. But he was claiming total ignorance.

"Close to becoming one. I approached her because I needed a decorator but we get along really well."

Hank began to brush off the cookie crumbs from his shirt. It looked like he was getting ready to make an exit.

"Shirley and Paddy are both great people. Very much in love. You must've seen them at the town meeting?"

Hank admitted he had not attended any yet.

"Paddy's an outsider too. Actually, so am I. They call us chicken neckers, you know. We should all stick together."

"Paddy sounds like an Irish name," Hank observed. "Never heard anyone mention him."

Jenny confided he was Australian. But of course he was of Irish origin.

"I'm surprised you never met him, Hank. He's very friendly. And so generous!"

A bell rang in the distance. Hank sprang up and told her he had to leave.

"No rest for minions like us."

Jenny gave him a tiny wave.

"It was nice meeting you, Hank. Welcome to Pelican Cove."

She stayed on the bench after he left, trying to gather her thoughts. It was obvious Hank Smith was lying. He may not have known Shirley or Paddy but there was no way he would be ignorant of Paddy's murder. It had been the talk of town for the past few days. One thing was certain. Hank Smith was hiding something.

The café was almost full when she got back. A few of her regular customers told her they loved the chicken salad. One man told her he found it very tart. The rest of the day passed quickly and Jenny drove home, feeling she had made no progress in finding Paddy's murderer.

She curled up with a book in the window seat up in her room, staring longingly at the ocean. Warm weather couldn't come soon enough. She missed going for a long swim.

Shirley called, wanting an update.

"Do you like the designs?" she quizzed. "And what about Paddy? When will the police arrest that woman?"

Jenny told her things were in motion, being vague on purpose. At this point, she wasn't sure of Shirley's innocence. Her reply didn't go down well.

"I think your reputation is overrated," Shirley retorted before hanging up.

With a wry smile, Jenny ambled to the kitchen, looking for something to nosh on. Jason was going to be home for dinner and she was looking forward to a quiet evening. She made a salad with spinach and baked some fish for their meal.

"How was your day, sweetheart?"

Jenny shook her head.

"No more talk of work. Let's do something pleasant, like plan a vacation?"

They both laughed. The café renovation meant Jenny would not be able to get away any time soon.

"We can go watch the cherry blossoms," Jason suggested. "Stay in the city for a day or two."

Jenny thought they could manage that.

They watched some television, lounging on the sofa side by side.

"Do you feel up to a walk?" Jenny stood up an hour later.

Jason declined, pleading an early morning meeting. Jenny laced her sneakers and wound a woolen scarf around her neck. The evening was cold and a bitter wind rattled the window panes.

"I won't go far. Just until my toes freeze in this wind."

They laughed. Jason told her she could take as long as she wanted. He would bank up the fire and make some hot chocolate.

Jenny's resolve wavered as soon as she stepped outside. But the button of her pants was a bit too tight and she needed to stay fit. She ran into Adam and Tank a few steps later.

Tank jumped up and placed his paws on her chest, giving a joyful bark.

"Get down, you beast!" she laughed, stroking his silky coat.

"Hey Jenny." Adam greeted. "Chilly weather."

Apparently not for everyone. She told him about her meeting with Hank. Adam could not stop smiling.

"That was quite ingenuous. Nobody could find fault with such a chance encounter."

It had yielded nothing, other than the fact that the new teacher in town was devious. Had Adam found out anything more about Paddy?

He paused mid stride, his hands in his pockets.

"Something's rotten here, Jenny. We ran a background check and it came back almost empty. There's barely any record about Paddy Benson anywhere. It's highly suspicious."

Jenny thought it wasn't that odd.

"Paddy's Australian, remember? He hasn't been in this country that long."

Adam frowned.

"What was an Australian doing in a backwater like Pelican Cove. Anyway, don't Aussies have an affinity for England? If one of them had to migrate somewhere, they would choose a place they were familiar with."

Jenny agreed with him.

"Paddy came here when he was a teen, hiked the Joshua Tree National Park. Ever since then, he wanted to spend more time in the United States, tackle some of the well known trails."

Adam pursed his mouth but said nothing. Jenny could see he wasn't convinced.

"And what about the man who was spying on Paddy?" she probed. "We know nothing about him."

Adam was sure Phyllis Tross had invented him.

"She was trying to throw us off. We have damning evidence against her, Jenny. I spoke to the medical examiner to get a better idea of the time of death."

"And?" Jenny sucked in a breath.

"Phyllis was there right around the time Paddy was killed."

Chapter 16

The weather turned for the better. Sunny skies smiled upon the islanders and they shook off some of their winter lassitude and stepped out of their homes. Jenny was surprised to see the café fill up just after Captain Charlie left. It was barely eight in the morning.

"We have a busy day ahead," Star noted, taking a carton of eggs out of the refrigerator. "How should we handle it, sweetie?"

Jenny decided to make a breakfast casserole along with a couple of extra pans of muffins. The ballots had been turned in and there was a buzz about what the vote count would reveal.

"Hello Mrs. Wilson," Jenny greeted the garage owner's wife. She was one of the regulars at the Boardwalk Café.

"What's made you venture out, the weather or the gossip?"

The woman had pasty skin and a round, plump face but a hearty laugh.

"A bit of both, Jenny. Peter told me you had come in." She leaned closer. "Have you made any progress in …"

Jenny told her she was working on it.

"There's a town meeting tonight," Mrs. Wilson continued. "You can bet there will be an uproar no matter what the votes say."

But what was the word on the street, Jenny wanted to know. Would there be a winter festival? That drew a knowing smile from the woman.

"I can't say anything right now. But there are bigger things cooking."

Jenny had to set the cryptic statement aside and get back to work.

With an instinct developed from running the café for the past few years, she came up with a menu that would please everyone.

"Mushroom barley soup, grilled fish sandwiches and chicken salad," she counted off her fingers. "And some chocolate chip cookies for those who want dessert."

Star questioned if it was too much.

Jenny glanced outside, her face lighting up when she saw the occupied tables in the dining room.

"They deserve it. Kind of a 'welcome back' to celebrate this fine day."

Star shook her head, setting out onions and celery on the kitchen table.

They chatted while Jenny diced the vegetables and a mound of mushrooms. The soup was boiling away soon and she made a quick sauce for the fish sandwich.

"Spicy mayonnaise." She added paprika and a good amount of Cajun seasoning. "Nick says it's all the rage nowadays."

The people of Pelican Cove could tolerate some heat in their food. This was the South, after all. So Jenny was sure they would appreciate the zesty condiment.

Star walked in and out of the kitchen, carrying food, bringing empty plates in.

"We are in for some trouble," she declared, sitting down to rest her feet. "I can sense these things."

Jenny dismissed her concerns. The crowd was riled up over the winter festival.

Betty Sue arrived, clutching her knitting bag to her bosom. Heather was right behind her, holding a skein of blue wool.

"You dropped this, Grandma!"

Ignoring her, Betty Sue gave them a wide eyed look and headed to the deck.

"I'd better check on her." Star followed them out.

Jenny brewed some fresh coffee and arranged some mugs on a tray. Heather came in, grumbling about nothing in particular.

"Can you take that?" Jenny pointed at a basket of muffins.

Molly came in, slightly out of breath. She didn't have a single book in her hands.

"You won't believe what I heard."

Jenny herded them all outside, eager to rest her feet and bite into a muffin.

Betty Sue and Star were deep in conversation.

"Are you objecting just for the sake of it?" Star spoke. "Many folks have been waiting for this. Everyone's tired of going to the Steakhouse."

Molly listened with rapt attention. Jenny surmised she had a good idea of what the old ladies were discussing.

"Where is this new restaurant going to be though?" Betty Sue sounded puzzled. "I am not aware of any land being sold. Anytime a property passes to a person who is not local, it must come to me for approval." She turned to Jenny. "That's what happened when you bought Seaview. Although Jason took care of all the paperwork, it had to go through me."

Heather pointed out the obvious.

"You're not thinking straight, Grandma."

This earned her an angry glare which Jenny thought was well deserved.

"Either there is no land being sold, which means a local is involved in this project. Must be a partner because even a lease would require your approval. Or ..."

"Or there is no restaurant," Jenny finished. "It's just a rumor."

Molly told them she had heard a few patrons talking about the restaurant in the library. It had taken precedence over the winter festival.

Jenny wondered if they would hear about it at the town meeting. She was curious to know why Betty Sue was against it.

"It's not going to help the islanders," she quipped. "Judging by all the tidbits I picked up, it's going to be an expensive place. They will hire skilled staff which will come from out of town. And so will most of their customers. No Jenny, this new restaurant will do nothing for Pelican Cove other than disturb our peace and spoil our environment. We already have a hard time keeping up with the tourists." She paused to take a deep breath. "12% of the island has been eroded in the past decade."

Molly rattled off a series of problems barrier islands faced. There was no doubt that increase in human traffic could compound their problems.

Heather gave a yawn and asked what Jenny was making for lunch.

"Yummy!" she exclaimed when she heard the menu.

Mushroom barley soup was her favorite as Jenny knew. And the hot mayonnaise also sounded like a treat.

"You can expect me back for a late lunch. I have to clean the rooms and take Tootsie for a walk but I'll be back!"

Jenny got busy preparing lunch after the Magnolias left. As expected, many people came in to grab a bite. A group of soccer moms arrived and ordered the soup, opting to eat half a sandwich because they couldn't resist.

"I'm doing low carb in the new year," one groaned. "But I can't resist this, Jenny."

Her friend mentioned the new science teacher.

"Mr. Smith may be smart but he's no oil painting, is he? Why couldn't he have been at least a bit handsome?"

Jenny remembered the woman was recently divorced. What would she say when she knew he was already taken? Hearing about the teacher set Jenny off on a spiral. She had no doubt he had been lying about not knowing Shirley. How could she prove it? Lying about being on a date wasn't a big crime. Many people did that, especially when they were cheating on their spouses. Was that the only reason for his perfidy though?

The crowd thinned and Jenny assembled a tray for herself, choosing a little bit of everything. She was glad Star had eaten earlier with Betty Sue, trying to coax her out of her temper. They had left for the inn a while ago, Star determined to make sure her friend stayed calm.

Jenny sat alone on the deck, reveling in the light breeze coming in from the ocean. She was very warm from being in the kitchen for most of the morning. She ate some of the soup, glad she could taste the pepper and garlic. The barley was just chewy enough.

A voice hailed her from the distance. Billy strolled up, dressed in his favorite outfit of khakis and a Hawaiian shirt, a sweater knotted around his neck. It had replaced the thousand dollar suits he had worn to work for most of his life.

"Hey Jenny! Mind if I join you?"

He came up the steps and sat before her, picking up the sandwich and taking a bite.

"Oooh! That's got a kick."

Jenny pulled the plate toward herself. She was hungry and there was precious little left.

"That's my lunch. If you want, I can make you a grilled cheese. But only after I finish eating."

Billy pulled the cup of soup toward him and ate a spoonful.

"Sure, sure. Anything that's easy." Then his eyes gleamed with hope. "You know what I'm craving right now? Those pineapple sandwiches you made for Nicky as an after school snack."

Jenny gave a fond smile, her mind traveling to a happy time. She cherished the memory of those days. Her son had never given them any trouble, getting high grades and staying out of scrapes. But he had been a bit spoiled.

"You remember that tantrum he threw when there was no pineapple once? It was after that big hurricane and I hadn't had a chance to do the groceries."

Billy nodded, then frowned.

"Are you out of pineapple right now?"

Jenny laughed and shook her head.

They finished the food on the tray and Jenny went in to make the pineapple sandwich. It had been her favorite too as a child. Her grandma always had them ready for her when she visited. Lost in the nostalgia, she couldn't help making one for herself too, then made an extra one, knowing Billy's hearty appetite.

He broke into a smile when she placed the plate before him.

"You know me well." He took a bite and went in raptures, wolfing down the sandwich. "What are you doing?"

Jenny had cut her sandwich in half, lifted a piece of bread and sprinkled some Old Bay on it.

"This is how new recipes are born," she quipped. "Won't know until I try."

Billy chose to stick to the classic.

"What were you thinking about when I came in?" His eyes narrowed as he looked at her. "Any new leads in that murder?"

Jenny poured her heart out, voicing all her suspicions about the science teacher.

"The kids worship him, of course. But I bet Hank Smith is not above board."

Billy wiped his mouth with a napkin, taking his time to chew his last bite. But his eyebrows had shot up. Jenny sat up, eager to hear what he was going to say.

"Did you say Hank Smith? Looks down on his luck, dresses in cheap clothes, limps a bit?"

"How do you know him?"

Billy leaned back and raised his arms above his head in a stretch. The corner of his lips lifted in a sneer.

"He's not a poor teacher."

"No, no. He is. I met him outside the school yard."

Billy corrected himself.

"I mean, he's not just a school teacher. The man is brilliant, Jenny. He may be the next tech billionaire."

Whatever Jenny had expected to hear, this wasn't it. She asked Billy to elaborate.

"Hank Smith is not just bookish, Jenny. He has business savvy."

He went on to tell her what he knew about the man. Billy had met him in the course of his work. Hank Smith had filed a patent for a one of a kind computer chip that would increase the speed of computing manifold. He wanted to manufacture it and was looking for investors. Based on the paperwork Billy had seen, he already had a lot of known people on board. He was looking for one last investor who would not only make up the difference, but also had a passion for science.

"He was quite firm about that," Billy told her. "This last financier would need to have more than just money." He paused, watching a seagull skim the waves. "Last I heard, he had approached a local man for that."

Jenny was astounded.

"The Newburys? I don't know anyone else in Pelican Cove who has some spare millions."

Billy gave her a knowing look. She caught on after a few seconds.

"No! Paddy Benson?"

"Bingo!" Billy slammed his hand on the table. "Supposedly, Paddy was impressed and was seriously considering it."

Jenny had a hard time processing this latest information. Billy had given her a lot to think about.

"Paddy owned a cattle station in Australia. Shirley hinted he wasn't stingy but I had no idea we were talking of millions." Then she paused a bit. "He loved the outdoors, of course. Told me so himself. Had a passion for hiking. But never said anything about science, Billy."

"Passion can spring when millions are involved." Billy shrugged.

Jenny clasped and unclasped her hands, slowly getting riled up.

"So this man lied to me about multiple things. He claimed he didn't know Shirley which is a blatant lie. And he acted as if he never heard of Paddy." She pressed her lips, staring at Billy. "Why?"

He told her it was kind of obvious. Hank Smith had a big motive.

"So he robs Paddy of both his money and his woman." Jenny mused. "He's playing a deep game, Billy."

Billy surmised he was not doing all that on his own. Shirley Brown had to be involved. Jenny realized he was right.

"I'm going to confront her today. She has one chance to come clean before I call Adam."

Chapter 17

Shirley welcomed Jenny with a watery smile and ushered her into a sunny room that could have come out of the pages of a magazine. The woman's flair as a decorator was evident. If she had actually done it herself, Jenny reasoned. She was beginning to feel skeptical about any skills Shirley possessed.

"Can I get you anything?"

An empty glass of wine reposed on a side table. Jenny couldn't tell if Shirley was just a bad housekeeper and hadn't cleared the dirty glass from the previous night. Or had she started to imbibe early?

"Whatever you like," she replied. "But no coffee, please. I'm just coming from the café and am already wired."

Shirley went in and put the kettle on.

"Let's have some herbal tea. I have a packet of chamomile languishing in my pantry."

Jenny asked how she was holding up. Shirley was in pajamas and wore no make up. She was playing the part of the grieving widow very well. Initially, Jenny had felt guilty about thinking like that but she was more cynical since new facts had come to light.

The kettle whistled and Shirley went in. She came out, holding a tray with two large stoneware mugs.

"I added honey."

Jenny told her that was fine.

"So?" Shirley picked up the mug and cradled her hands around it. "Have you found something? Oh Jenny, Paddy was such a force of nature. I miss him!"

A light creak sounded in the background, startling Jenny. Was there someone else in the house? She couldn't help feeling jittery. In her mind, she knew Paddy had been murdered at a different location, but she thought of this place as the 'murder house'.

"I can still feel him around," Shirley echoed her thoughts. "As if he'll walk in through that door with an armful of flowers and hand them over to me." She paused, lost in a memory. "He was crazy about flowers!"

Jenny let her talk, encouraging her to share anecdotes from her life with Paddy. It was a subtle way of gathering information. People often revealed a lot about themselves when they were not on their guard. Shirley might admit things she had kept close to her chest so far.

"You met Paddy," she sighed. "As if he was not attractive enough to look at. He had this way of making you feel wanted. When Paddy showered his attention on you, you felt you were the only person in the world."

Jenny had an inkling of what she meant.

"He seemed taken with the Boardwalk Café. That picture he painted of having one in every town on the coast, that's a pipe dream. Was he involved in any other business deals at the moment?"

Shirley shrugged. He was retired but the entrepreneurial spirit ran in his blood. He liked to dabble here and there.

"Paddy had plenty of money. He had a lot of respect for anyone striking out on their own. I never took an interest in that part of his life though."

Jenny felt Shirley begin to close up. She steered her to more pleasant subjects.

"You met on a hike, didn't you? Must have been odd at first, going out with a foreigner."

Shirley lifted a finger, asking her to hold on. She disappeared inside and came out, holding a platter of corn chips and salsa.

"It's over an hour since I ate something."

Jenny sampled a couple of chips, fanning her mouth. The salsa was hot!

"I'm from New Zealand," Shirley began. "Born and brought up there but came here on a backpacking trip. Never went back."

Jenny scooped up more salsa with a chip, urging her to continue.

"I did the odd job here and there ... waitressing, bagging groceries ... nothing steady, you know. Then I took a job as a trail guide, working for a company that arranged hikes for rich people. That's where I met Paddy."

"Wasn't he a lot older?"

"He was! Around twelve years older, but he thought it was twenty." She cracked a smile. "A woman can lie about her age. It's not even perjury."

Jenny refrained from comment.

"We had a lot of things in common," Shirley continued. "He had been to New Zealand many times and I'd also spent some time in Australia. We grew up eating the same foods, like Vegemite. Both of us had an ancestor in England."

Jenny got the idea but she let Shirley ramble.

"Why did you never get married?"

Paddy had proposed a couple of times but Shirley didn't really believe in the institution of marriage. She came from a broken home and was skittish.

"We signed a contract every six months," she chuckled. "I told Paddy it would keep us on our toes. Either of us could walk out when it ended."

Jenny got the chance she was looking for.

"Were you thinking of leaving him?"

Shirley's eyes flashed fire.

"Why would you think that?"

"You did say you might be leaving town," Jenny reminded her.

"Oh, that!" Shirley dismissed, but provided no more explanation.

Jenny glanced at a clock on the wall. She had been there for over an hour. It was time to grab the bull by the horns.

"How do you know Hank Smith?"

Shirley's face was blank.

"Who? I think I've heard that name somewhere but I'm drawing a blank."

Jenny told her he was the new science teacher at the high school.

"Right!" Shirley sat up and ate the last chip on the platter. "One of the moms in my book club was talking about him. Not a very exciting character, she said. But the kids like him."

Had she never met him, Jenny persisted. Shirey did a flip and agreed they had been introduced at the school fund raiser.

"He's the kind you wouldn't spare a second look, but now I remember." She frowned. "I think I saw him walking on the beach once. He waved and I waved back."

Jenny was surprised to hear that. Shirley's account was very different from Hank's. He denied knowing her at all. That meant the two had not rehearsed their stories. Did that mean they were not colluding? Had the murder been a crime of passion, a spur of the moment thing, maybe. There was no denying that Shirley's fingerprints had been found on the weapon. Her involvement could not be overlooked. Was it possible Hank had no inkling of what she had done?

Forcing herself to stay quiet about the fingerprint, she told Shirley she had to leave.

"I saw Phyllis in her garden this morning. When are the police taking her in?"

Jenny answered with a shrug. The police worked on their own timeline. She wasn't privy to it.

"They might be waiting for a warrant. Just be patient and sit tight."

She told her about the town meeting and asked if she was going. It would provide some distraction. Shirley wasn't sure she wanted to face people.

"It's a good idea but I can't bear the thought of people gossiping about me."

She needn't care about that, Jenny reasoned. Shirley smiled and promised to think about it.

"I will breathe freely once they arrest Phyllis," she sighed. "It's a bit scary, living next door to her. How do I know she won't pop in and stab me in my sleep?"

Jenny was speechless. Shirley was laying it on too thick. She said goodbye and drove back home, analyzing her visit and going over every word Shirley had said. By the time she reached home, she hadn't been able to form any specific opinion about the woman.

Star sat in the living room with Jimmy Parsons. They were watching The Three Stooges.

"Howdy Jenny!" Jimmy greeted. "Your aunt is worried about you."

Jenny spent some time with them, then went out for a walk. She needed to clear her head and go over what she knew so far. Phyllis Tross had fought with Paddy and was present at the house where he died. Was her motive strong enough though? Did her garden mean more to her than a human life?

Hank Smith was the real enigma. He had lied about multiple things. His interest in Shirley was a puzzle. Had he just been trying to sweet talk her to get close to Paddy? Based on the story Billy brought, Hank needed Paddy's money for setting up his new business. That meant he would gain nothing from the man's death. In fact, Paddy's death would be a major setback to his plans. Maybe he was just being careful and wanted to keep a lid on any plans until they came to fruition. She could understand that. Jenny herself did not like to count her chickens until they were hatched.

And what about Shirley? Jenny was convinced she had been after Paddy's money. How much did she gain from his death? Adam was working on that.

Had Paddy been gullible enough to leave all his assets to Shirley? She tried to imagine Shirley ingratiating herself to him over the years. If she'd been really canny, she would have married him. Anything Paddy owned would automatically have passed on to her in that scenario. But that wasn't the case here. Legally speaking, Shirley had no rights where Paddy was concerned. So was she smart or stupid? Jenny could not decide.

She got back home and took a shower, dressing warmly to go out. The town meeting was bound to be more interesting than usual that night.

Star had already left with Jimmy. Jason called and said he would be a bit late. He was going to meet her at the town hall.

Jenny got into her car, watching a sprinkling of clouds travel across a pink sky. The sun was creeping close to the horizon and it was a glorious sight. On a whim, she pulled up by the side of the road and stepped out, leaning against the hood to take in the view. She waited long after the golden orb dipped below the water, enjoying the kaleidoscope of colors the sky was dishing up.

A nagging thought bothered her on the way to the hall. Was it something Heather had said? Jenny couldn't help but feel that she was missing a vital detail. She parked the car and walked to the entrance in a daze, barely noticing when Jason hailed her.

"Hello!" He tapped her shoulder and embraced her. "You're frowning."

Jenny told him it was nothing. They went in and walked to the front row. Star, Jimmy, Heather and Molly sat in a line with two empty seats next to them. Jenny's mind clicked when she saw Molly.

"I'm trying to remember what you said about Paddy." She groaned. "That's kinda vague, isn't it?"

Molly beamed, patting the space next to her.

"Not at all. I asked about the man who rented that beach house. The one where Paddy's body was discovered."

Jenny gaped, her mouth hanging open.

"Of course! What was Paddy doing there, huh?" She turned to Jason. "I don't believe this is random."

He placed his arm around her and nodded.

"You can meet this man tomorrow. Now let's enjoy this, shall we?"

Chapter 18

Jenny hardly noticed the time the next day. She prepped for lunch, waiting for Molly. They were going to review some design ideas for the café. Molly arrived, brandishing a large tome.

"I started a scrap book."

Jenny was amazed at the amount of effort she had gone to. Then again, it was just like Molly. She had carefully photo-copied ideas from several magazines going back years, cut out pictures and pasted them in the book.

"I think we should go for something classic. No bold or hot styles because they go out of fashion pretty quick."

Jenny agreed with her. She did not plan to redecorate every year or two.

"The art will be the focal point, as we decided. And we can rotate those, changing the look. Star will provide whatever we want."

They worked in tandem, agreeing on almost everything and finalized the concepts for all the rooms. Now Jenny had to hire a contractor who would be able to realize her vision.

"So, the town meeting last night," Molly said. "What do you think of a new fancy restaurant? You and Jason go out a lot, don't you? This will be convenient."

Jenny wasn't sure. They had a few favorite places along the Eastern Shore that they liked to visit for date night. She realized driving out of town and getting away from the usual places was part of the charm.

"Betty Sue is not in favor of the idea. And it's all very vague. I think someone floated the rumor just for the sake of some free entertainment."

They laughed. It had happened before. The winter lull could get quite boring.

Molly left soon with a brown bag Jenny pressed in her hands. It was lemon and herb chicken salad that she had liked before. Jenny was making grilled fish salads for lunch. She assembled a dozen salads in bowls and marinated some bass fillets, feeling the time was dragging that day.

She had been wracking her brains since morning, mulling over Shirley and Hank. What should her next step be? The only idea she could come up with was crazier than any she'd had before. Adam would probably lock her up and the Magnolias would also not be in favor of it. Maybe Heather would approve and want to go. Or would she?

The lunch hour kept her busy. Some of the customers were talking about the town meeting. She felt gratified when she heard more than one person agree that the proposed new restaurant was just hot air.

Star took their food out to the deck. Jenny cleared up a bit and joined her.

"This Asian dressing is so good!" Star licked her spoon. "Is this a new recipe?"

Jenny admitted she had sneaked in a few Sichuan peppers. They were supposed to have a numbing effect on the tongue but the amount she had used was miniscule.

"What are your plans this afternoon?" she asked her aunt.

Star wanted to go home and rest. Jenny urged her to go ahead. She would stay back a while and clean up.

"I'm right behind ya."

She tried to brush away the guilt she felt for the white lie. But Jenny did not want anyone to accompany her on her stakeout. That's what she was going to do that afternoon, keep an eye on Shirley's house. Or Paddy's, to be precise.

Half an hour later, she set off in her car, wondering if she would find an empty spot on the street. When she reached her destination, she realized she had not anticipated the real problem. The street was deserted and she stuck out like a sore thumb. Anyone in the four or five houses in the vicinity who happened to glance out would be able to see her.

Pulling on a pair of dark glasses, she shielded her face with a newspaper and slid lower in her seat. A sudden giggle escaped. Jenny was aware what she was doing was completely out of character. She had never set out to break into anyone's home before this. But she had a strong hunch that the answers to some of her questions lay inside that house.

An hour passed. She saw Shirley strolling through the house, moving from one window to the other. The woman was dressed in a robe, much to her chagrin. There was a fat chance she was going to leave the house. But Jenny's prayers were answered some time later. Shirley stepped out, dressed to the nines in a short black dress and matching heels with red soles. She got into the late model luxury car in the driveway and pulled out. Jenny bent down, hoping Shirley wouldn't recognize her car.

She waited five minutes, then got out of the car and crossed the road. The locals never locked their doors. But Shirley and Paddy were both outsiders. Thinking there was no harm in trying, she checked the front door. It was locked. Placing her hands on her hips, Jenny looked around, contemplating her next move. She decided to walk around the house, looking for an open window.

There was a lot of glass but no window she could pull up. Daffodils bloomed in the garden next door.

"What are you up to?" A terse voice demanded.

Jenny whirled around and faced Phyllis Tross who was pointing a pair of garden shears at her.

"Some shenanigans, no doubt."

Jenny took a quick decision.

"The police might arrest you any minute, Ms. Tross."

"You're bluffing."

Jenny decided to show her cards.

"We know you drove to that house where Paddy was murdered. What were you doing there?"

"Following him."

Did she realize it placed her at the scene of the crime? Phyllis protested, her jaw quivering with indignation. She was innocent. She believed there was a possibility Paddy stole flowers from other gardens. The rented bungalows were an easy target, especially when they were empty.

With a start, Jenny realized Phyllis could be right. But she needed the woman to feel pressured.

"One way to evade arrest is to help me find something to implicate Shirley."

That spurred the woman into action. She had a spare key. Paddy had given it to her when he first moved into the neighborhood.

"It was before he started stealing my flowers," she growled. "Wait right there. Don't move!"

Jenny tapped her foot, thirsty. It would be too much to hope for some hospitality from Phyllis. Thankfully, the woman was back in a jiffy and handed her a key.

"Good luck."

Jenny stared at her back, then spurred into action. She had no idea how long Shirley would be gone.

A quick stroll through the house gave her a general idea of the layout. There was a large open kitchen and family room in addition to the formal living area Shirley had met her in. A flight of steps led upstairs from the kitchen. Jenny surmised all the bedrooms were upstairs. She spotted a closed door and went in, thrilled to find it looked like a study or office. There was a large manager's desk right in the middle of the room, with a plush leather chair. Bookshelves lined the wall and a large picture window looked out onto the yard behind the house.

Taking a deep breath, Jenny sat in the chair and began pulling out drawers. She had no idea what she was looking for and was relying on pure instinct. There were boxes of pencils and pens in one, along with some unused legal pads. Another had stacks of envelopes, stamps and a third was overflowing with tiny stuffed toys, the kind people kept on their desks. A kangaroo fell out and Jenny picked it up and put it back in.

Unwilling to give up, she turned to the other side, banging her knee in her haste. The top two drawers were empty but she persisted and hit pay dirt in the one at the bottom. There was only one object in there, a thick book bound in cloth. Had Paddy kept a journal?

Jenny grabbed it and began rifling through the pages.

"Oh!" she exclaimed. "An appointment book."

There were random entries with dates in the left column. Some were mundane, probably dinner dates with Shirley or meetings with his business contacts. Jenny recognized the names of restaurants in Virginia Beach and Washington. A few cryptic entries made her smile. They mentioned flowers, just a date and a type, like roses or tulips or daffodils. Jenny didn't care if they referred to orders he had placed or blooms he had stolen from Phyllis. Her hands stilled when she reached the last page.

Paddy had made an appointment for the day he died. He was meeting someone that morning, at the address where his body had been found. It mentioned a name and time and in a tidy scrawl below that, three words that made Jenny sit up. 'This ends today!'

Jenny sprang into action, snapping photos of the offending text with her phone. She also took some random pictures of other entries in the book. Then it was time to leave. Sucking in a breath, she crossed her fingers, hoping she would be able to escape before Shirley got home. She felt a draft when she stepped out of the room. Walking further down the passage, she saw that the patio door was open. Five minutes later, Jenny was back in her car and speeding away from the neighborhood.

The sky had darkened while she was in Shirley's house, the black clouds a harbinger of an incoming storm. Jason was home. He greeted her with a hug and took her to task.

"You've been playing truant."

Jenny promised to reveal all after she had slipped into something more comfortable. They stood in the kitchen, sipping wine while Jenny made dinner. Jason stopped in the process of tossing the salad when she showed him the photo she had taken.

"I think you have a breakthrough."

"Yes and no. We have no idea what this means."

After a dinner of Shepherd's pie, roasted beet salad and warm berry pie, they lounged in front of the television, watching a thunderstorm light up the sky.

Rain fell in torrents and Jenny thought she would have to miss her walk.

"Adam is not going to be happy," Jason warned her. "You broke your word again, Jenny."

She would have, she argued. But Phyllis had handed her the key. So technically she had entered by the front door.

"Without Shirley's permission," Jason gently reminded her.

Jenny chose to believe she had Shirley's blessing, since she was the one who had urged her to find the truth about Paddy's death.

The storm passed quickly and the rain let up. Shaking off her lethargy, Jenny laced her sneakers to go for her walk.

"You coming?"

"No, I'm going for another slice of cake."

Jason ran five miles on the beach every morning, a luxury Jenny did not have. But she looked forward to her walks.

She encountered Tank just outside her garden gate.

"Have you been waiting for me?" Jenny rubbed his ears and hugged him close.

Adam stood at the edge of the water, his feet planted apart, watching them. Jenny sensed he was about to berate her.

"Will you never listen?" He sighed. "What if someone had walked inside that house and trapped you?"

Had Phyllis babbled, Jenny wondered. Or some other neighbor? It didn't matter. She brushed off his concerns and told him what she had found.

"Do you know anyone called Harris?"

Adam didn't respond right away. He began walking away and Jenny fell in step with him, Tank running a few feet ahead.

"We had a deal, Jenny. You can't go off like this without keeping me in the loop. Not on my watch."

She apologized, realizing what a fool she had been. What had prompted her to take such an irresponsible step?

"Harris?"

"He's the man who was renting that bungalow."

"Wow!"

Molly was right.

"But here's the disconnect," Adam reasoned. "Judging by the note, Paddy is the one who intends to harm him."

They considered a few scenarios. Maybe the two men had argued, there was a fight and this man Harris killed Paddy in a fit of anger.

"I talked to Shirley too," Jenny added, relating what she'd said about Hank Smith. "Their stories don't match."

Adam thought it was a good sign. It meant Shirley and Hank were not in collusion.

"Or they are and they gave us different stories to make us think that."

Adam's lips spread in a smile. She wasn't taking anything for granted, which was good.

"Come with me to meet Harris."

"You bet," Jenny beamed. "Come to the café for breakfast."

Chapter 19

Jenny was excited the next morning. This was the day they would crack the case. She diced vegetables for omelets and decided to make pancakes. It had been a while since she made any.

Captain Charlie was waiting outside when she opened the café doors.

"Good morning, Jenny." He beamed. "Do I smell chocolate?"

She laughed and told him to take a seat.

"One stack of chocolate chip pancakes coming up."

He rubbed his hands in glee. There was no charter that morning and he wasn't going out on the water. So he had time for a leisurely breakfast. Jenny urged him to take a seat and went back to the kitchen. She loaded a tray with a stack of hot cakes, an extra cheesy omelet and toast, adding crocks of butter, strawberry preserves and a small jug of syrup.

"Any progress?" Captain Charlie asked, cutting into his omelet.

"I think I'm getting closer." It was all Jenny would admit but it made her feel better.

She certainly knew a lot more than she had at the beginning. That had to be a good thing.

Heather arrived, her face glowing with happiness. Jenny raised her eyebrows, an unspoken question on her lips.

"Billy and I went out last night." She picked up a piece of toast and began buttering it. "That's all I'm saying right now."

It was a move in the right direction, Jenny thought. But she was silent, reluctant to push Heather in the other direction. She made the chicken salad, started a pot of vegetable soup and decided she would fry some wings later.

"What kind of sauce should I make for the wings?"

"Something with a kick," Heather said at once. "But a bit sweet. Try something new."

Jenny had been thinking of a recipe. There was no time like the present.

Heather made herself a batch of pancakes and sat in the kitchen, digging into them. Star and Adam arrived almost at the same time.

"You can leave any time, sweetie. I will handle things here."

Jenny made two egg white omelets with spinach and mushrooms and took them out. She and Adam ate quickly.

"Ready for this?" he asked.

"Where are we going?"

"Not far! My boys made some inquiries. Harris is holed up at the motel."

Where else? Jenny should have thought of that before. He must have gone there on purpose, to be around plenty of people to build an alibi.

They set off, Adam warning Jenny to stay a step behind him and let him take the lead.

"I'm responsible for your safety." He locked eyes with her. "Whether you're sitting in my patrol car or not."

The motel perched on the edge of the bridge leading out of town was very familiar to Jenny. The unctuous manager fawned over her, offering coffee.

"We are here on police business," Adam interrupted in a stern voice. "You have a guest called Harris?"

The manager almost trembled but he gave a nod.

"Take us there."

Adam rapped on the door. It was opened almost immediately, by a short, balding man dressed in a hideous yellow shirt. The strains of a cartoon track filtered out. Jenny thought it sounded very familiar, then smiled when she recognized it.

"Harris?" Adam quizzed. "We have some questions for you."

"Ain't done nothing wrong." The man's frown turned into a snarl.

Since Adam was wearing his Sheriff's uniform, there was no need to announce he was from the police. But he introduced himself as a matter of form.

"I'm Adam Campbell, the Sheriff of Pelican Cove. I need to question you about the dead body in your house. You can talk right now or accompany me to the police station."

The man moved away from the door, reluctantly signaling them to come in.

"Not my house," he spat before Adam could say anything more.

There was only one chair in the room. Jenny sat in it. Harris perched on the edge of the bed and Adam remained standing. The manager hovered near the door.

"You can leave us alone," Adam ordered. "And close the door behind you."

He turned to face the man.

"Full name, please."

"Rio Harris. Do you wanna see my ID?"

Adam ignored the sarcasm and fired some routine questions to establish he was the man who had rented the house in question.

Jenny's eyes had been roving around the room. She was familiar with the layout, having been involved in solving a murder at the motel before. There was a small duffel bag on the luggage rack. Other than that, there were no personal items lying around. She stood up on the pretext of using the bathroom.

"You can't spy on me," Harris glared. "Who's the chick?"

Adam warned him to be quiet and asked him to narrate what had happened.

"I needed some quiet time," he began in a sullen tone. "Doctor's orders. So I rented this house in the middle of nowhere. My buddy's girlfriend came here last summer and couldn't stop whining about goin' back."

Adam told him to move on.

"Well, it was peaceful. No complaints there. Hardly saw anyone around. Got fresh fish at the market every day. Dined like a king and lazed around in a hammock all day."

In short, he had been enjoying his furlough. Then the heat stopped working one morning. He placed a call to the owner and asked him to get it fixed.

"Man told me he would be there pronto. But guess what? I waited all day for the fella to turn up but no luck. Then I booked a room here at the motel and came here. No way I'm spending the night without a heater. In the middle of winter too."

Jenny thought there were many holes in his story. Yes, it was winter and Pelican Cove was experiencing a colder season than usual. But it wasn't that bad, surely? Couldn't the man have gone for an extra blanket?

"Where are you from?" She couldn't stop herself.

"Upstate New York." He puffed up. "We're more civilized over there."

So he came from a colder clime.

"Did you know Paddy Benson?" Adam moved along.

"The dead man?" Harris twisted his mouth in a sneer and shook his head. "Of course not. Never heard of him."

Adam asked if he had received any threats. Harris shook his head, his eyes bulging out of their sockets. There was no doubt the question had thrown him.

"For what? I wasn't in anyone's way."

"We found some evidence that Paddy Benson had a meeting at your bungalow that morning. He intended to, how should I say it, end things."

Harris declined having set up any meeting. He had come to Pelican Cove to be away from people.

"What is your line of work, Mr. Harris?" Jenny probed.

He owned a garage. They shot a few more questions at him but he didn't break down or reveal anything pertinent. Harris maintained he had never gone back to the place after that evening. In fact, he had no inkling of what happened there until he had heard the maids gossiping in the passage outside his room.

Adam turned toward Jenny, his frustration clear. She shook her head. There were no other questions she could think of at that moment.

"Don't leave town without my permission," he ordered Harris.

"When can I go back to my place?" the man queried. "I got more than a month on my lease."

Adam replied they would let him know.

"Tom & Jerry?" Jenny pointed at the muted TV on her way out. "I love them too."

Harris gave a grudging nod and shut the door after them.

They drove back to the café after convincing the manager they did not have time for coffee. Neither of them spoke for a while.

"That wasn't very helpful." Jenny burst out. "I know it's not right to judge a person by his appearance but ..."

"He looked like a thug." Adam cut her off, the hint of a smile lurking on his mouth. "Acted like one too."

First impressions were often right. She was a sleuth now and she had to trust her intuition. The police would run a background check on Rio Harris as a matter of routine.

"I won't be surprised if he has a past record."

Jenny admitted her eyes had strayed to the open wardrobe. There were no clothes hanging inside. Clearly, the man had arrived at the motel in a hurry and did not intend to stay more than a day or two.

Had Paddy made an error in his appointment book? Maybe he had noted the wrong address.

"And he was killed because of that?" Adam was incredulous.

There was a lull at the café. Star offered to make fresh coffee. Adam thanked her and said he wouldn't mind a muffin to go along with it.

They sat on the deck, going over everything again. Jenny asked if they had found any other fingerprints in the house.

"None other than Paddy's," Adam replied. "And Shirely's. It's as if Harris was never there."

Maybe he was right, Jenny considered. Had anyone actually seen Harris living at that bungalow? That led her down a path that made no sense.

"It's winter," she mused out loud.

"Yeah Jenny," Adam replied drily. "I think I'm aware of that."

Star brought their coffee and beat a silent retreat, sensing the tension.

"What I mean is, this is the time when there are almost no tourists in town. Paddy's lived here long enough to know this is a slack time. Most of these new houses are booked solid in the season but there is no demand for them right now. In fact, one can almost guarantee they are empty."

Adam sipped his coffee and encouraged her to go on.

"I think Paddy must have asked Shirley to meet him there, anticipating that there will be no one around. He intended to confront her about Hank Smith. I think Paddy found out, was enraged and of course, he felt cheated. He must have been planning to break up with Shirley."

"Couldn't he do that in their own house?" Adam refused to buy her theory.

"Not if he intended to harm her, Adam. He brought up Hank Smith, didn't get a suitable reply from Shirley and attacked her. She must have fought back to save herself."

Shirley had grabbed the closest weapon at hand, a kitchen knife, and the worst happened.

Adam picked out a blueberry from his muffin and gave a deep sigh.

"I hate to disappoint you, Jenny. But you're overlooking an important detail."

"What?"

"Paddy mentions Harris by name in that appointment book. No, Jenny. He went there to meet the man. Shirley may have accompanied him, or she followed him there for some reason."

Jenny wasn't willing to give up her theory easily.

"And they squabbled? The situation turned ugly and Shirley stabbed him in self defense."

Adam scratched his jaw, his eyes narrowed in contemplation.

"Or she saw it was a golden opportunity to get rid of him and killed him in cold blood."

Chapter 20

Jenny's phone rang. It was Nick.

"Hey baby!"

"Guess what, Mom. I'm heading south on I-95. Should be there soon."

Jenny cried out in delight. This was an unexpected surprise. She had been longing to meet her son, secretly hoping he would at least visit for a short while that weekend. Billy had told her it was difficult.

"How did you manage it? Your father said ..."

"I'm working tomorrow. Will have to take some calls and attend an online meeting. The client's on the west coast in Oregon. So my boss agreed I might as well visit my sick mother."

Jenny asked what was wrong with her. Nick had been vague, hinting at mysterious womens' ailments.

"Gives me plausible deniability."

"Spoken like a lawyer!" Jenny answered fondly. "You just made my day, bubba. Can't wait for you to get here. But drive safely, okay?"

Nick promised to take a couple of stops and stick to the speed limit.

"How is she, Mom?"

They both knew who he was talking about.

"I think she's coming around. Your father took her out last night."

Both agreed it was a positive sign. But Heather hadn't opened up. Jenny thought they were not resolving anything by brushing her issues under the carpet.

Nick promised to talk to her and hung up.

Adam was watching her, a smile softening his stern features.

"Nothing beats that feeling, huh. The girls have not been home in a while and I miss them."

Jenny inquired after Adam's twin daughters. There was a time when she had considered being their mother. Nick and the girls were good friends and Jenny lavished her affection on them whenever they came home to visit.

They were both lost in thought for a minute.

"Are you going back to the station?"

Adam paused, then shook his head. It was a fine day and he was in a mood to get some air.

"Why don't we go talk to Shirley Brown?"

Jenny couldn't believe it. She asked him to give her a few minutes to powder her nose. True to her word, she was out almost immediately, her bag slung over her shoulder.

"This is my lucky day."

Adam was not the kind to share his strategy. Jenny tried to think about ways he would handle the questioning. Was he going to be calm and laid back, or would he confront her head on and accuse her of Paddy's murder?

They stopped in front of Shirley's house. Jenny's gaze traveled to the garden next door. A few more daffodils had bloomed in Phyllis's garden.

She got out on her own and followed Adam, taking care to stay one step behind.

"You see I can follow orders?" she teased and tapped him on the shoulder.

They both noticed the front door at the same time. It was ajar.

"Stay right there, Jenny!" Adam warned. "This is highly suspicious."

Was it really, Jenny thought. Shirley must have forgotten to shut the door. Maybe both her arms were occupied, carrying groceries, and she just shoved it with her shoulder or hip. Adam was jumping to the wrong conclusion.

"Let's wait here for a minute," she urged. "There may be a simple explanation."

He nodded, but kept one hand on his holster, using the other to ring the doorbell. Two minutes passed, then five. Shirley did not appear. Jenny felt a frisson of concern. Her eyes flew to Adam's. There was no need to say anything.

Adam forged ahead and knocked on the door, announcing himself. With great effort, Jenny forced herself to stay where she was. He was back two minutes later. She heard the sirens before he caught her eye and shook his head.

Jenny feared the worst.

Two police vehicles screeched to a stop on the street, followed by an ambulance. Adam's deputies began following his orders. One of them took her by the arm and gently led her to a car.

"Sheriff's asked me to give you a ride, Ma'am."

In a daze, Jenny thanked him and told him to drop her off at the café.

"What happened?" she blurted. "Is Shirley dead?"

The man told her he was sorry. He could not divulge anything.

The Magnolias sat on the deck of the café, deep in discussion about Heather's date.

"Does this mean you are engaged?" Betty Sue's eyes were filled with raw hope.

Heather told them they were rushing ahead. She and Billy had just talked.

"You've been doing that for the past year." Betty Sue sighed. "This is not right, Heather. Don't string the poor man along."

Molly spotted Jenny.

"Hey! Are you back already? Star said you went out with Adam."

Three pairs of eyes swung toward her. Star acted first. She was by her side immediately.

"Take a load off, sweetie. Looks like you've had a shock."

Molly's eyes grew larger behind their soda bottle lenses.

"Wait. What? What's happened?"

"Shirley's gone. I'm guessing it was deliberate. The police are there right now."

Her mind registered a few random phrases she had overheard and she connected the dots.

"I think she was stabbed with a knife, just like Paddy."

There was a stunned silence. Heather sprang up and went in to make some fresh coffee. Star urged her to eat something.

"I'm fine," Jenny insisted. "Or I will be, in a minute."

Molly told her she couldn't blame herself. There was no way she could have anticipated that Shirley was in any danger.

"She was a suspect, wasn't she?"

Jenny nodded, thinking about Shirley's prints on Paddy's murder weapon.

"We went there to question her. I think Adam was convinced she was guilty. He was prepared to arrest her."

Heather came out, holding the coffee in one hand and a plate of cookies in another. She poured a cup for Jenny and added cream and sugar.

"This is why you should keep some hard liquor on hand," she joked. "Are you sure there isn't any vodka under the sink?"

Jenny barely heard her. But she knew Heather was keeping up some chatter to distract her. One by one, they all started talking about the winter festival.

"There will be a town meeting today to declare the results," Betty Sue spoke. "No winter festival this year."

Molly asked if that decision was based on the votes. Was it the popular opinion or had Betty Sue vetoed the results?

"Doesn't matter. And there will be a strict warning to whoever is floating those silly rumors about that fancy restaurant."

Nobody had applied for permission. That meant it was all hot air.

"You think it's these new people?" Molly mused.

Heather thought it had been an indirect way of sounding them out, gauging the local opinion. Why spend millions on a business that has no demand?

Jenny let their words roll over her, watching the waves crashing on the shore. A seagull screeched in the distance. She got up and stood by the railing, staring at the horizon, her mind blank. Thoughts returned one by one. Shirley had been so full of life but she had lied about something. Jenny wondered why the woman hadn't confided in her.

"She should've told me." She mumbled.

Molly and Heather came to stand beside her. They wrapped their arms around her waist, offering silent support.

"Why didn't she say anything?"

"Don't blame yourself," Molly begged. "You tried to help her inspite of the contrary evidence."

But why would anyone murder Shirley, Jenny wailed. It made no sense at all.

They led her back to the table.

"Paddy and Shirley," Jenny wondered out loud. "Both murdered within a few days of each other. There must be a thread connecting these two deaths."

Molly thought they all knew the answer. It was obvious Hank Smith was involved. It was a lovers' spat.

"Hank wanted Shirley for himself so he killed Paddy. Either on his own or with Shirley's consent."

Heather thought it had to be without her knowledge.

"Hank may be obsessed with her. Maybe Shirley liked him but wasn't ready to take the next step. He wanted to help things along. So he murders Paddy, then waits for Shirley to jump into his arms. It doesn't happen. The poor fool owns up to what he did. Shirley is shocked and breaks up with him. I mean, she was kinda brassy. That's what I admired about her."

She came up for breath. Jenny continued her line of thought.

"Shirley must have caught on to Hank Smith somehow. She confronts him, or decides to do a bunk. It's the ultimate betrayal for Hank. He flies into a rage and kills her too."

"Yes!" Heather and Molly cried in unison.

Jenny agreed the idea had some merit. The police would have to question Hank.

Molly reminded them of the other possibility.

"What if Shirley and Hank were both involved in Paddy's murder? They can ride into the sunset now and there is no need for Hank to hurt Shirley."

Jenny's head had begun to throb but she forced herself to concentrate.

"Do you mean there is another killer out there? Who?"

Heather slammed the table with her fist. They had all forgotten the other mysterious man. The one Phyllis Tross had talked about.

"According to her, he spied on the house and followed Paddy around. But Paddy and Shirley were often together."

Molly beseeched her to come clean.

"Just spit it out, Heather."

"Well, we thought this man with the binoculars was spying on Paddy but what if he was after Shirley?" She stared at Jenny. "We know nothing about her."

Jenny opened her mouth to tell them about Shirley's background. But Betty Sue beat her to it.

"Enough!" she boomed, flinging her needles on the table. "That's just enough, girls." She pointed her finger at Jenny. "You! We almost lost you last time. Do you ever spare a thought for the people who worry about you? Jason, and Star. And Nick, your son. Billy." She waved a hand around the table. "And us! Not that we are connected by blood."

The next thing she knew, Jenny had her arms around Betty Sue.

"You're my family. Of course I care about you. How could you even doubt that?"

Heather, Molly and Star had left their seats and gathered around the two of them. Tears streamed down every face. Jenny didn't actually make any promises but Betty Sue assumed she had given in.

"No more sleuthing!" she cautioned. "Let the police do their job for once. That Campbell boy needs to earn his pay."

Nobody said a word after that. Heather stuffed the knitting in a tote and followed Betty Sue out of the café. Molly muttered something about getting back to work. Star was the only one left beside Jenny.

"It's time to start lunch."

Jenny took a deep breath and followed her into the kitchen. Molly had forgotten her scrap book on the table. Shirley would never give an opinion on the designs.

She switched on the fryer and pulled the marinated chicken wings out of the refrigerator. The thoughts churning in her mind would not abate. She was convinced that the two murders were connected. If Paddy had been the target, Shirley had been caught in the middle. She was an innocent victim.

What had Shirley Brown done to provoke the killer?

Chapter 21

Jenny went on a cooking spree. Her son was coming home after a long time and she wanted to give him a proper welcome. She made big bowls of pimento cheese and crab dip. Captain Charlie had dropped off some jumbo shrimp. She would fry them in a butter garlic sauce just before dinner. There was pot roast and roasted sweet potatoes. And she would make a big flan for dessert. Nick always loved what she cooked but he would also provide constructive criticism.

Feeling she had things under control, she went up to take a bath. The enormity of the day's events hit her. She wanted to hide under the covers and go to sleep. But she couldn't do that to Nick. He was driving all the way from the city, just to meet her.

Jason opened a few bottles of wine after he got home. They would have company, of course. Nick arrived and swept Jenny up in a hug.

"How are you, Mom? Really?"

Heather had called him to give a heads up.

"I don't mind if you want some time to yourself. Dad and I can go to the Rusty Anchor. Or we'll order pizza and I'll stay with him."

Jenny shook her head.

"You're not getting out of my sight. Dinner's almost ready."

Jason clapped him on the back and offered him a can of beer.

"Your mother's been frantic. It's been a while since we saw you."

Billy arrived with Heather and Betty Sue on either side. Star brought Jimmy and Captain Charlie. And the party began.

Jason proposed having a barbecue the next evening. He went out and built a fire in the pit. Everyone trooped out to the garden.

Jenny did not notice the time pass which was good for her. She came to a decision before she turned in to bed. There was no point in putting off the renovation. She would call the Cohens the next day and ask them to start work as soon as possible.

Morning came quickly. Jenny rushed through her routine and drove to the café, excited about cooking breakfast for her son. She was making crab omelets and chocolate chip pancakes, his favorite.

Captain Charlie took muffins to go. Jason and Nick came in together and urged Jenny to eat with them.

"Don't forget your mission," Jenny reminded her son. "We really need to resolve this."

Nick promised her he was on it. He was going on a drive with Heather to check out some of the beaches he hadn't been to.

"Dad wanted to come but she brushed him off. She said 'No old fogeys.' And then she told me she wanted to spend some quality time."

Did that mean Heather was going to confide her worries in Nick? She crossed her fingers and wished him luck.

It was Friday and Jenny was frying fish for lunch. She made tartar sauce and was roasting peppers to make hummus for sandwiches when Adam strode in.

"Good morning!" he greeted. "Can you tell me something about that voyeur?"

Jenny replied in the negative, then gave him the solution.

"I know a person who can though."

With the lunch prep done, Jenny had some free time. She suggested they go and talk to Phyllis Tross.

"She might be more amenable in her home."

She talked Adam into driving to the garden center just outside town on the state highway. Then she took her time buying some bulbs of tulips. They were on sale.

"Why are we here, Jenny?" Adam didn't hide his irritation.

Jenny asked him to be patient. They drove to meet Phyllis after that. She wasn't out in her garden but one of the white lace curtains in the sun room window twitched. Jenny was convinced she was inside.

"You lead the way," Jenny told Adam. "She can't slam the door in your face."

"That's what you think," he smirked. "These old ladies are a law unto themselves."

Jenny hoped the woman would be more forthcoming, now that both her annoying neighbors were dead. But she wouldn't hold her breath for any basic hospitality.

Phyllis answered the door, dressed in a sweater set and pearls, a pale pink lipstick slathered on her lips.

"Are you going somewhere?" Jenny burst out.

Pressing her mouth in a firm line, she asked Adam what he wanted.

"I would like to ask you some questions, Mrs. Tross. The police need your help."

Her mouth settled in a smirk and she invited them in.

"You were a rambunctious child, you and your brother. Gave your mother a lot of trouble."

Jenny asked Phyllis how she was and handed her the bag from the garden center. She confessed she wasn't an avid gardener.

"Hope it's not too late for these."

Phyllis took the bag, a faint blush appearing on her cheeks. She informed Jenny that every inch of her garden was planned in meticulous detail. There was no space for the tulips.

"Where am I going to put them?"

"I was sorry to hear about all the damage your garden suffered." She saw the surprise on the woman's face. "You spoke about it at the town meeting."

"Oh, okay. Thank you."

They took their seats in the living room, Adam and Jenny sitting on a sofa while Phyllis perched on a chair with spindly legs.

"What do you want to know?"

Adam asked her to describe the man who had been watching Paddy's house. How often had she seen him? Since when?

"Almost every day," Phyllis replied. "For the past couple of months. Wait, I noticed him after Thanksgiving, I think."

She had gone to visit one of her kids and stayed with them for a week. When she came back, she found him standing in her flower beds.

"I read him the riot act, of course," she bristled. "He just left without an apology."

Jenny asked her to describe him.

Phyllis told them he was quite tall. Six feet or more would be her guess. He had golden blonde hair and eyes as blue as a summer sky.

"Not hard on the eyes," she relented, "but absolutely no manners."

Adam wanted to know when she had seen him again.

"Two days later," Phyllis replied promptly. "He was in a beat up car on the other side of the street. But he still had that camera around his neck."

"Camera?" Jenny quizzed. Hadn't she mentioned binoculars?

"Did I?" Phyllis frowned. "No, it was a camera."

He was there come rain or shine, parked in different spots. The cars changed too. She had even seen him at night, long after the lights in Paddy's house were extinguished.

Jenny asked if he still came to spy on the house. Phyllis took her time to answer.

"I did see him after Paddy passed. Just once or twice, mind. He hasn't been around since."

Jenny tried to hide her disappointment. All this was very vague, hardly enough to locate the man. They didn't even have a name.

Phyllis surprised her by offering to make tea. Adam said nothing. Jenny realized they didn't really have a choice.

She followed the lady into her kitchen, offering to help. Gleaming copper pots hung from hooks. Blue gingham curtains fluttered in the window. Pots of herbs lined the sill. Suddenly, Jenny realized what a beautiful home Phyllis had. It had that quintessential Southern feel, the one she wanted for the newly redecorated Boardwalk Café.

Phyllis pointed at a porcelain jar and instructed Jenny to place four cookies from it on a plate. She did as she was bid and followed Phyllis out to the living room.

"I don't know if Betty Sue mentioned this ..." she began. "I'm renovating the café. We came up with some designs and the work should start soon."

Phyllis told her to get on with it.

Jenny explained how she wanted to preserve most of the old look, just spruce it up a bit.

"Petunia put her heart and soul in it. I don't wish to erase her legacy." She picked up a cookie. "It would be a big favor to me if you helped me select the fabrics and the new furniture."

Phyllis looked like she had died and gone to heaven. Her face beamed in a broad smile, making her look friendly for the first time.

"With pleasure, my dear. We all associate a lot of nostalgia with the Boardwalk Café. I'll make sure you don't lose that."

They drank some tea and left. Adam grinned at her when he started the car and drove away.

"Really, Jenny? You want Phyllis Tross to help you?" He shuddered. "Flowers on the curtains and the upholstery?"

Jenny pointed out that the only flowers in the house they just visited reposed in vases. Hadn't he noticed the many diverse elements around the room and how well they blended together?

Adam told her he trusted her judgement. He stopped outside the Boardwalk Café.

"So that wasn't very helpful, huh?"

Adam told her he had enough to work with. He would circulate the man's description to his team and ask them to track him down.

"He's an outsider, Jenny. Someone's sure to have spotted him."

The Magnolias sat on the deck, waiting for an update. Jenny drank her coffee and told them about her offer to Phyllis.

"What about us?" Heather cried. "This is such an insult."

Betty Sue approved. Phyllis Tross was a thorny character but she had good taste. Many of the ladies in the knitting club sought her advice for decorating their houses.

Many people came to eat the fried fish and Jenny stayed on her feet until she ran out of most of the food. Star had saved her a sandwich.

"Jason's called off the barbecue. He has a late meeting in town. But he promised to get Chinese food."

Would Nick be disappointed? He had been hard at work himself all day. She called Billy and told him about the change in plans.

"Why don't we take our boy to the Steakhouse?" he offered. "Loaded baked potato, cherry cobbler, big T bone ... he likes that!"

Jenny told him to ask their son what he wanted. He wasn't a child any longer. Maybe he had made his own plans.

Jenny dragged herself up to her room after she reached Seaview. She stood in the window overlooking the ocean and stretched, trying to work the kinks out of her neck. She spotted Nick in the distance. He had gone for a run on the beach.

She went down and made a tropical smoothie for him, adding frozen mangoes, pineapple and a fresh banana. Then she added some coconut cream.

The screen door leading to the garden opened and Nick came in, drenched in sweat.

"Is that for me?" He kissed Jenny on the cheek. "You pamper me, Mom."

"That's my job, son."

She asked if he wanted a ham sandwich, then told him the barbecue was off.

"I don't mind," he assured her. "Actually, I'm going to take this up to my room and catch up on my sleep. Wake me when Jason gets home with the food."

Jenny wouldn't mind a nap herself. She started to wipe down the counters and told Nick she was right behind him.

The phone rang when she had just switched off the light and taken a step into the passage outside.

"Hello!"

"Jenny, it's me. Adam, I mean. Adam Campbell."

She waited with bated breath. He would not call unless he had an update.

"My men found him, the man Phyllis talked about."

Jenny felt a surge of energy as she waited to hear more.

"He calls himself Johnny Finch. Fortyish. Looks just like she described. Rents a room with one of the locals."

What was he doing in Pelican Cove, Jenny wanted to know. Had he owned up to shadowing Paddy? She could imagine Adam shaking his head.

"Claims he's a bird watcher. Here on an extended vacation because of his health. The camera is to take photos of the birds, of course. Showed some to my deputy. Hundreds of geese, duck, herons and fowl."

"Do you believe him?"

"No, I don't. That's why I'd like you to go talk to him."

Chapter 22

J enny couldn't sleep that night. They had enjoyed a family dinner after Jason got home. He brought Chinese food from Jenny's favorite restaurant. Surprisingly, Nick partook of the feast with gusto.

"Don't you order a lot of Chinese when you're working late?" Jenny teased. "I thought you must be sick of it by now."

"It's not the same." He pointed at his plate, loaded with beef broccoli, fried rice and an egg roll. "Leong's is the taste of nostalgia."

Nick suggested going for a walk after they ate. Jason pleaded fatigue and headed up to his room. Jenny sensed her son was about to share something important.

They bundled up in warm coats and set off. A chilly wind ruffled Jenny's hair and made her cheeks sting. She waited until they were a few paces away from the house. Jason appeared in their bedroom window and waved.

"What is it, Nicky? Tell me quick."

"I can't hide anything from you." He groaned. "Heather said a lot. She didn't extract a promise to keep it to myself. So my guess is, she actually wants me to tell you this."

Jenny was intrigued. Heather was known for speaking her mind. She had never hidden anything from Jenny.

"You got my attention."

Nick cleared his throat, looking a bit embarrassed. He confessed he didn't know how to sugar coat it. Jenny urged him to spit it out. She could handle the truth.

"Heather believes Dad is still in love with you."

Jenny's eyebrows shot up and she was stunned into silence. This couldn't be. Heather believed Jenny was the other woman in her relationship.

"But ... but ... that's impossible!" She swallowed. "Non sense!"

Nick was silent.

Jenny poked a finger in his arm, forcing him to speak.

"I don't know, Mom. She could be right. Dad misses us being a proper family. He talks about our old life, a lot." He folded his arms and turned around to face her. "Why do you think he moved to Pelican Cove? He wants to be around you."

The Magnolias had talked about this. After a brief affair with a young woman, Billy had come to his senses. Part of his soul searching had led him back to Jenny. He had befriended all of them, including Jason. And they had all accepted him into their circle.

"I love Jason," Jenny sighed. "And I'm going to spend the rest of my life as his wife. Your Dad knows that. More importantly, he accepts that. He would never have started dating Heather otherwise." She was growing incensed. "And Heather knew our history before she started going out with Billy."

Nick nodded along. He had been giving it some thought. What had spooked Heather?

"She's feeling insecure. I told her she has to take a leap of faith. No matter who she dates, Dad or anyone else, there will always be an element of uncertainty."

When had her son grown so wise?

"Heather needs to confront Billy. Let the poor man know why he's being strung and quartcred."

That's what Nick had told her. Heather promised to do it. She needed a day or two to drum up the courage.

"I'm sorry to burden you with this, Mom."

Jenny hastened to assure him it was fine. But her mind was in turmoil.

She was just falling asleep when her alarm rang at five. Forcing herself to get ready, Jenny drove to the café, determined to put on a strong face.

Captain Charlie greeted her with a wide smile when she opened the café doors.

"Good morning, Jenny. It's a fine day, isn't it?"

Jenny glanced at the dark clouds lining the sky and the fog in the distance and shrugged. Captain Charlie followed her in and stood by the cash register, tapping a tune with his fingers on the desk.

"Well, it's about to get better, Missy."

"Are you eating here?" She gave a yawn. "I'm making eggs to order today."

Sensing her mood, he paused, his brows drawing together in a frown.

"What's bothering you, dearie? Are you worried about the renovation? We already decided I'll come to Seaview for my breakfast."

Jenny shook her head, feeling her eyes sting with tears.

"I'm calling the contractors today. The kitchen won't be closed for long, maybe three or four days tops. I'll deliver breakfast to the regulars. Not you."

Captain Charlie asked for scrambled eggs with cheese. He followed her into the kitchen.

"Whatever's troubling you, it's best to just talk about it. I'm not saying it should be me. Your aunt or your husband will do. Or your friends."

Jenny tried to crack a smile but failed. She was quiet while she made the eggs just as he liked them, sprinkled some Old Bay on top, and set the plate before him.

"Will you keep me company?"

The café was deserted so Jenny poured some coffee for herself and agreed to join him on the deck. Captain Charlie buttered a piece of toast and handed it to her.

"Have a bite."

She thanked him and bit into it, chewing it on autopilot.

Captain Charlie sampled the eggs, declared they were the best he had eaten and stared at her with a twinkle in his eye.

"I was going to wait until I was done eating but I think you need cheering up."

In her wildest dreams, Jenny couldn't have imagined what he was going to say next.

"I saw that new teacher yesterday, the one you gals have been talking about."

"Hank Smith?"

Captain Charlie nodded. Hank had been standing on the bridge, staring down at the water. The boat inched toward the bridge, giving Captain Charlie a good view of the man. For a second, it had looked like he was going to jump.

"I slowed down, just in case. The shock of losing his woman might have addled his mind."

The Captain hadn't been completely wrong. He saw Hank Smith lean forward and drop something in the water.

"Do you know the exact spot?" Jenny sprang up and began to pace the deck. "Captain Charlie, what if you took me there?

Would you be able to fish it out? And how big was this thing anyway?"

She came back and put her hands on the table.

"This is highly suspicious, don't you think? If the man wants to dispose something, he can put it in the trash. Why go all the way to the bridge and dump it in the water?"

"Calm down, calm down. Take a load off."

Jenny couldn't believe he was grinning. Did he even realize the gravity of what he had seen?

"I did you a solid, Jenny." He laughed and explained he had anticipated all her questions. "I hung around the bridge for some time, giving the man time to leave. Then I fished it out."

He had the package! Jenny was so excited she couldn't breathe.

Captain Charlie rooted in the rucksack by his feet. He carried it slung over his shoulder every day and Jenny had barely paid any attention to it.

"Here you go." He pulled out an oblong, cylindrical object and placed it on the table.

It looked like something one used to store tennis balls. The tube was wrapped in a shiny plastic, or an oil cloth. Jenny extended her hand to touch it, then paused. Would it have finger prints? Then she reasoned Captain Charlie had already handled it.

216

"I'm speechless! This could be a big clue. It might help us build a case against the man." She frowned. "But how do we know it's not just some piece of trash? He may just be a litter bug."

"I don't think so. This was anchored with some heavy stones. Your teacher wanted to make sure it sunk to the bottom of the bay and stayed there."

Jenny thanked him for his effort.

"Tell me what you want for lunch. My treat."

"How about those chipotle chicken quesadillas?" he winked. "With extra cheese."

Jenny gave him a high five and promised she would be waiting.

True to her word, she marinated the chicken in adobo sauce, counting the minutes until Heather or Star would come in.

"Finally!" she cried when Star arrived, wearing a paint splattered smock.

"What is it, sweetie?" her eyes clouded in concern. "Are you feeling well?"

"Never better."

Jenny promised to be back soon and left at a clip, clutching the object Captain Charlie had handed her. She set a record pace for the police station and barely glanced at the person at the counter, giving her a slight wave.

"Adam!" she hollered. "You in there?"

She gave a knock on the door marked 'Sheriff' and pushed it open, confident he wouldn't censure her. Not when he saw what she'd brought in.

"Hello Jenny!" He leaned back in his chair and tented his hands together.

She set the object on the table with a flourish and sat, trying to catch her breath.

"What's this?"

Adam had chosen this day to be infuriatingly calm.

"A smoking gun!" Jenny crowed. "That's what it is. This will help us nail Hank Smith."

Curious, Adam straightened and asked her what the package contained. She answered with a shrug and narrated everything Captain Charlie had told her. He warned her not to get her hopes up. But he wasn't completely indifferent.

Jenny returned to the café at a more sedate pace.

The Magnolias were on the deck, speculating about the reasons for her absence.

"There she is!" Molly patted the empty space beside her. "Where did you rush off to?"

Once again, Jenny recounted everything that had happened that morning.

"Hank Smith better watch out. I think he'll be arrested by the end of this day."

She was greeted by silence. Betty Sue stopped knitting and began with a shake of her head.

"I asked around. That man's a very good teacher. And he's a lamb."

She shared an anecdote about how he'd stopped a kid from bullying a girl. If any student failed an assignment, he always gave them a second chance in the form of a makeup test.

Molly added the gossip she had picked up at the library. When the school's entry was rejected at a well known science competition, he cried with the students.

"Frankly, Jenny, I don't see how this guy could hurt a fly. And you're saying he murdered two people."

They all stared at her, waiting for her to fall in.

"What about that man Phyllis told us about?" Heather demanded.

Jenny realized she hadn't told them about him.

"Turned out to be a bird watcher," she sighed. "The police already questioned him. There is no way to connect him to Paddy or Shirley."

None of them had any new suggestion. The best course of action was to wait and watch what the day revealed.

"It all depends on what's in that tube like object Captain Charlie fished out of the water." Jenny accepted she was stumped. "Meanwhile, I'm going to make quesadillas. How many of you are staying for lunch?"

Chapter 23

Jenny devoted herself to making the chicken quesadillas she had promised. Unable to do anything in a half hearted manner, she made guacamole to go with them. She should have felt good about finding evidence that would nail the teacher. But a nagging feeling at the back of her mind would not let her rest.

Nick was heading back to the city. Jenny packed some quesadillas for him. He came in and hugged her tight, promising to drive safely and stop at a rest area to eat.

"Will you be careful?" he reproached. "I'll be back soon, Mom."

Captain Charlie came in, did justice to the food. As usual he was very generous in his praise. Betty Sue and Heather had also stayed back. Fortunately for them, there was not much of a lunch crowd. It meant there was plenty left for them.

"You don't look pleased," Heather observed. "What's bugging you, Jenny?"

"Ready for a quick trip?"

She realized she did not know where the bird watcher was staying. But she was loathe to call Adam. He would advise her to leave well enough alone. She turned to Betty Sue for assistance.

"Can you find out where this guy is putting up? Finch is the name, I think."

With a shrug, Betty Sue agreed and made a few calls and set things in motion. They lingered over the coffee, waiting for the phone to ring. In half an hour, Jenny had the address she wanted.

"Where is this place?" she asked.

"Way out, near the horse farm," Betty Sue replied. "Barb Norton's cousin lives there. Keeps chicken and goats, grows her own vegetables. She's more eccentric than your typical islander." She cackled. "Might set you to work, collecting eggs, if you don't watch out."

Jenny wondered if this was the day when her friend had chosen to be humorous. She stared back for a second, watching for a smile to emerge but there was none.

"She's not kidding." Heather whispered.

"You coming for a ride?" Jenny quipped. "Just give me some time to clean up in the kitchen."

The bright afternoon was warm and pleasant, perfect for spending some time outdoors.

Heather wanted to know why Jenny was wasting her time.

"Hank Smith will be in police custody soon. What do you want from this bird watcher?"

"No harm in covering all the bases. We don't know what's in that tube like thing Captain Charlie fished out. Maybe it won't be enough to arrest Hank."

There was another point bothering her. What if Hank Smith had not killed Paddy? The man was going to invest in his venture. Hurting him would not aid him. Hank might have got Shirley out of the way because of some lovers' tiff. In that case, they would still need to find out what happened to Paddy.

They reached a small ranch style building set on a large tract of land. The gates were open, embedded in mud. They looked like they had been like that for years. Jenny spotted a chicken coop behind the house. A goat bleated in the distance.

"Kinda sparse," Heather voiced. "Where does this woman have space for a lodger?"

They got out of the car and walked toward the door. Jenny pointed at a structure behind the chicken coop. It looked like a small shack or tool shed.

"Is it possible?"

Heeding Betty Sue's advice, they took a circuitous route to the shack, hoping they would escape Minnie Norton's eye. The door to the shack was painted a bright blue.

Heather banged on it with force. If there was anyone inside, they would not be able to avoid answering it.

Jenny felt some relief when the door swung open. A tall, blonde man with deep blue eyes stared at them, a wry smile on his face.

"Ladies!"

Adam's description had been accurate. The man had an imperious manner, arrogance oozing out of every pore.

"Can we come in?" Jenny inched forward and peeped in.

There was a duffel bag on the bed, beside a few folded clothes. A camera sat on them. Finch was about to flee. They were just in time.

"How can I help you?"

Jenny pointed at the bag on the bed.

"Are you tired of Pelican Cove? It can be quiet for a young one like you, especially in the winter."

He hastened to correct her. If he had his way, he would love to stay on.

"There's a certain magic about this place. I have never encountered so many different species of birds anywhere. Some of the pictures I took will fetch me a good price. But I have to get back to real life."

Jenny asked about his pictures.

"That's why I'm here, actually. You see, I am redecorating my café and am looking for some ways to feature the best of the Eastern Shore and the island itself. I thought of having a wall dedicated to the local birds. Would you be willing to sell some of your pictures?"

Heather butted in, telling him it would be better if he donated them.

Finch moved across the room, subtly shielding his bag with his body.

"Why not? Anything for the Boardwalk Café, huh? It's one of a kind, Ma'am."

He went on to praise the food Jenny cooked. Nothing could rival her prowess in the kitchen. If there was one thing that would bring him back to Pelican Cove, it was Jenny's food.

That brought Jenny to her senses. She had never seen him before and was positive he had never come to the café. So the man was bluffing but why? She took a few steps to the left, trying to keep him engaged in conversation. Why was he covering the bag? Had he stolen something from Paddy's house?

She locked eyes with Heather for a second, hoping she would catch on.

"Where do you go from here?" Heather asked. "I don't think you live by the water."

Jenny tried to stand on her toes with an intent to peep into the bag. Something glinted. The hair on her arm stood up. Was it possible? She inched closer, pretended to sway and let herself drop on the bed.

"Ow! Ow, ow, ow." She screamed.

Finch pushed aside the duffel bag and took her hand, pulling her up with force.

"What happened, Miss Jenny? Did you faint?"

She closed her eyes and clutched her temples, letting out a small groan. It was as if a bolt of lightning had passed through her leg, she said.

"I don't know. My knee buckled and I lost my balance."

Heather surmised she had missed breakfast.

"You need to eat something."

Finch offered her a can of soda. That was all he had on hand. There was no vending machine since he wasn't living in a proper hotel.

Jenny took the can, popped the lid off and took a few gulps. She thanked him for his care.

"This will do for now, I think. But I better get back to the café. You will send me the photos? I can have them printed in the city."

Nodding vigorously, he ushered them to the door, closing it as soon as they stepped out. Jenny grabbed Heather's arm and pulled.

"What was that?" Heather whispered.

"Let's just get out of Dodge first."

They set a rapid pace for the car. Heather chose to drive and Jenny didn't object. There was a shout and a woman came out of the main house.

"That must be Millie Norton." Heather turned the key in the ignition and stepped on the gas.

The tires spun and they sped away, holding their breaths until they cleared the gates and saw them recede in the rearview mirror.

"He has a gun!" Jenny cried. "I saw it peeping out of that duffel but I wanted to be sure."

"That's why you pulled that silly stunt." Heather's voice was full of admiration. "Where do we go now?"

Jenny asked her to drive straight to the police station. She needed to talk to Adam. It was necessary they apprehend Finch before he bolted.

"But Paddy was stabbed with a knife," Heather argued. "So was Shirley."

Jenny pointed out that ordinary people did not carry guns in their luggage. Finch was no bird watcher. He had come to Pelican Cove with an agenda.

They reached the station a few minutes later and Jenny wasted no time running in. The woman at the front desk warned her to wait.

"Sheriff's in a meeting, Miss Jenny. Not to be disturbed."

"This is urgent! Could be a matter of life and death. Can you please ask him to come out and speak to me for a minute?"

The desk sergeant wasn't pleased but she pressed some buttons on the phone and said something. It must have been some code because Jenny didn't understand a single word. The door to Adam's cabin flew open and he rushed out, looking harassed.

He sighed in relief when he saw her.

"You're in one piece! What's wrong, Jenny?"

"Johnny Finch is carrying a gun. I saw it myself."

Adam's eyebrows shot up.

"You went alone?" He ran a hand through his hair, mussing it up. "You promised!"

Heather had come in by then. She assured him she had been there with Jenny. Adam stared back at his cabin. He was in the middle of interviewing Hank Smith. But he promised to send some deputies to round up Finch.

"The man must have been up to some mischief. We'll find out soon enough." He took a deep breath. "Why don't you go back to the café for now and let the police handle this?"

Chapter 24

J enny turned around to leave but Adam tapped her on the shoulder, asking her to hold on. She couldn't hide her surprise when he led her to an empty office and asked her to sit.

"Can I get you anything? Some water, or soda?"

Heather had followed them in. She let out a low whistle.

"What's with the warm hospitality, bro? I thought you were booting us outta here?"

Adam answered with a glare but said nothing. He turned back to Jenny, asking her how she was feeling now.

"Is Jason in town today? I'm going to give him a call."

Jenny's heart was thudding in her chest but she had barely realized it. Adam was very solicitous. He assured her she was not in any danger and urged her to calm down.

"Take deep breaths." Heather stroked her back. "We've got you, Jenny. I'm beginning to wonder if that fainting spell was real."

Adam's eyes popped out when he heard about the elaborate maneuver Jenny had performed to establish the contents of the bag.

"You're one of a kind. But there is no need to panic."

Jenny admitted she had been frightened. She was just beginning to realize it.

The desk seargent brought coffee. It was lukewarm and burnt but sweet. Jenny wrapped her hands around the mug and thanked her for the warm drink. Cajoled by Adam and Heather, she took a few quick sips.

She finally asked about Hank Smith.

"Have you arrested him?"

Adam nodded. Captain Charlie's package had yielded the goods. They had found a knife coated in blood, wrapped up in a sheaf of papers.

"The prints have been identified as Smith's. And I'm sure the blood will belong to Shirley Brown. We are waiting on the lab results to confirm it."

So Hank Smith had confessed to stabbing Shirley?

Adam told her that's where the problem was. He claimed to be innocent.

"The teacher agrees he handled the knife. He says he went to Shirley's house and saw her lying in a pool of blood. The knife was sticking out of her. He reached for it and pulled it out. It was an instinctive action."

Why had he dumped it in the water then, Heather quipped. Jenny could guess how he would answer that.

"He panicked?" she asked.

Adam told her she had hit the nail on the head. Hank Smith realized he would be in big trouble. So he fled the scene, carrying the knife. He later decided to dump it in the bay so it could never be found and traced back to him.

Jenny asked if he believed the man.

"Like you said, Jenny. It's a smoking gun. The prints on the knife cannot be overlooked." He scratched his chin. "Do you suddenly think this man is innocent?"

Jenny paused, trying to collect her thoughts. Adam was right, of course. What had made her give Hank Smith the benefit of the doubt?

"It's Finch. I stared into those cold blue eyes of his, Adam. He lied effortlessly. If I had to choose between the two of them, Johnny Finch is more likely to be a criminal."

Adam was trying hard not to laugh.

"I've never known you to take an instant dislike to anyone. This Finch guy has really raised your hackles."

Heather agreed he looked wily. But was he capable of murder, she couldn't say either way. He must be prepared to be violent, if he was carrying a weapon.

"The police believe in hard evidence. Let's hope Smith is our man because otherwise we'll be starting from scratch again."

Jenny asked about the papers he had mentioned. What did they contain?

"Some business plan and some bank documents," Adam dismissed. "I was about to ask him about them when you arrived, Jenny. My guess is he just used whatever was on hand to wrap the knife in.

Jenny finally smiled. Hadn't she told Adam about Hank Smith's patent?

"Hank Smith's an innovator of sorts. Billy knows someone who was working on his behalf. Smith was looking for investors in his business. In fact, he had approached Paddy for it."

Adam found it all very suspicious. Why would anyone come to a remote small town like Pelican Cove to get funding? They would go to California, or New York or Boston, places known for fomenting technology startups.

"We're running a detailed check into his background and finances. It should yield something. Now, if you permit, I would like to continue my interrogation."

Jenny dropped Heather off at the Bayview Inn. She came out almost immediately. Star and Betty Sue were at Seaview.

"Mind if I come too?"

Jenny admitted her nerves were shot. She couldn't shake the jitters that had been with her since she met Finch. Heather suggested going out for drinks later.

"Not a bad idea," Jenny agreed.

The older ladies were relieved to see them. Star couldn't stop frowning as Jenny related everything.

"He had a gun? You placed yourself in danger again, sweetie!"

"Well, he didn't threaten us or anything. So it's possible we had nothing to fear from him."

Star thought they had spent enough time dwelling over crime. She wanted to let her hair down for once and get away from it all.

"And I'm not in a mood to cook."

Jenny echoed her sentiments. It had been a long time since they had gone out of town.

"Let's go to Virginia Beach. We can go to that games arcade, stroll along the boardwalk and grab a bite somewhere."

Her idea was met with approval. Even Betty Sue cheered up, ready to stretch her legs. Jenny called Molly and went up to take a shower and dress up.

"You can borrow something from me," she told Heather.

The sun was setting when they piled into the car and headed out of town. The sky was ablaze in bright hues. The deep blue water of the Chesapeake Bay surrounded them as they traversed the seventeen mile long bridge that would take them to the mainland of Virginia.

It was an evening to remember. They played every possible game in the arcade and won hundreds of points. Jenny exchanged them all for a small stuffed toy. Then they bickered over who would get to keep it.

Molly was craving Asian food and they ate at a Mongolian barbecue, trying out crazy combinations of sauces and spices. Then it was time to go home.

Jenny had a restful night and woke on time the next morning. She was filled with anticipation of what the day would bring. Had the police uncovered any more evidence against Hank Smith?

She made the chicken salad, slid muffins in the oven and beat eggs for the omelets. Captain Charlie stood outside when she flung the doors open.

"Good morning, Jenny!" He beamed, following her in. "Have an early charter today so I can't dawdle."

She packed half a dozen muffins for him along with a thermos of coffee.

"That item you fished out is going to make a big difference. The police should give you a medal, Captain Charlie. I'll talk to the Sheriff about it."

He burst into laughter and walked out, giving her an airy wave.

Adam came in two minutes later. His face was a mask of stone and Jenny knew there was trouble.

"What happened?"

"Can I bother you for a hot breakfast, Jenny? Barely got any sleep last night."

She nodded and invited him to sit wherever he wanted. He chose the deck. Five minutes later, Jenny took his omelet and toast outside, along with coffee. She had made the same for herself.

Adam sat in a corner, partly shielded by a potted plant. Thick clouds covered the sky and rain was predicted, making the atmosphere sultry. Jenny sat, anxious to hear what had happened through the night.

"They were all fake," Adam began, cutting a tiny piece of his omelet. "Those financial papers we found in that package. The business plan, the funding received from the investors ..."

Jenny's mouth hung open. What did he mean?

"Hank Smith is no whiz kid. And he hasn't invented a darn thing."

The police had confronted him with what they found in the background check. Hank Smith had come clean.

"He was a science teacher in a small town in Indiana. Got hooked into some shady business, a land scam that Paddy was running. Hank put all his money into it and was bankrupted when the deal went south. Unable to handle the shock, he tried to commit suicide."

Jenny stirred sugar in her coffee, listening in rapt attention.

"That limp he has ..."

Adam nodded. The man had jumped off a building and hurt himself badly. But he didn't die. He spent years in recovery, living on welfare. A cousin of his moved to the Washington, DC area and invited him for a visit.

"This is all so fantastic."

"There's more." Adam buttered his toast and took a bite. "So he's in the DC area, it's summer, and what do they decide to do?"

Jenny shook her head. She had no idea.

They had come to Pelican Cove to spend a day at the beach.

"Guess who Hank Smith spotted in our little town?"

"Paddy?"

Adam slammed his fist on the table.

"Yes, the man who destroyed his life and made it a living hell."

Fueled by a burning desire to seek revenge, Hank Smith looked for a job in Pelican Cove. He had only one goal. Con Paddy the same way he had been conned, and fleece him for enough money so he could send his son to college.

"Diabolical," Jenny cried. "And that's a strong motive! Did he confess?"

Adam told her Hank Smith admitted he was trying to swindle Paddy but he maintained he was innocent of murder. He had never intended to cause physical harm to anyone.

Shirley must have caught on to him somehow. Is that why he had silenced her?

"Actually, he has a strong alibi. An unshakeable one."

Adam sipped his coffee and rubbed his eyes. The medical examiner had given the time of Shirley's death. Smith was at school that whole time, taking a class. Dozens of students were a witness to that.

Jenny wondered why he had gone to the trouble of wrapping up the knife in such an elaborate manner, then dumping it in the water. Adam had asked Hank the same thing.

"He panicked," Adam replied. "Grabbed the first thing at hand. I can believe that. Even an innocent man loses his mind when faced with murder. Smith never imagined anyone would see him on that bridge." He took another bite. "Assuming he's innocent, he didn't know when Shirley died. So he had no idea he would have an alibi."

Jenny chewed her omelet, barely tasting anything. All her efforts had produced nothing.

"We're back where we started. But what about those dates with Shirley? What was the purpose of that?"

Adam set his knife and fork down and shook his head, looking defeated.

"He befriended her to get closer to Paddy. They were in cahoots, Jenny. We can only guess what Shirley's motivation was."

Jenny's thoughts were in a whirl. Did they have any other suspect? Was Phyllis the guilty one after all? Her thoughts flew to the gun she had spotted in Finch's luggage. He had been caught snooping and shadowing the victims and he had a weapon. But did he have an alibi for the times the murders were committed?

Adam read her mind easily.

"We have Finch in custody. In fact, I'm going to interrogate him as soon as I leave."

"Can I …"

With a sigh, Adam pushed back his chair and stood up.

"Alright, Jenny. At this point, I'll take any help I can get."

Chapter 25

J enny felt some apprehension, walking to the police station with Adam. She did not trust Johnny Finch. There had been something elusive in his manner, a sneaky look in his eyes. He was a chameleon, someone who changed at the snap of a finger as it suited him. They needed to establish if he was a criminal, one who had committed the ultimate crime.

"You are not afraid?" Adam sensed her mood. "I'll be there with you. And you can be sure this man will be unarmed."

Jenny thanked him for his concern. Of course she had nothing to worry with him around.

They entered the station and went directly to the small room Adam used to question or interrogate people. Johnny Finch sat there, cool as a cucumber. His eyebrows went up when he saw Jenny, and his mouth settled in a smirk.

"What is this woman doing here?"

"Never mind that!" Adam chided. "Dare I remind you we have brought you in on suspicion of murder? It's time for you to come clean and start talking."

Finch lifted a shoulder in a shrug and claimed he had nothing to hide. He goaded Adam to ask him anything. But first he wanted a drink.

Adam raised his hand and gave a subtle signal. Jenny realized they were being recorded. A seargent came in a few minutes later, carrying three paper cups of coffee. Finch took a sip, declared it could be worse and folded his arms, staring at them in defiance.

The man appeared very confident, Jenny observed. Was that because he was innocent?

"Let's begin with where you were when Paddy Benson was murdered."

He mentioned a date and time span and waited for Finch to respond.

"On my own, watching the birds." He cackled. "Not in a bar or any public place. So I don't think anyone will be able to vouch for me."

Adam asked about the day Shirley had been murdered. Finch frowned, gave it some thought, and shook his head.

"Same. No alibi."

Adam told him he'd had enough. Finch seemed to deflate. His insouciance evaporated and he shrugged, giving up on his whole act.

"I have a permit for that gun, Sheriff. As I have no doubt you have discovered by now. And I'm a licensed private investigator."

Jenny exclaimed loudly. Out of all the reasons she had allotted for Finch's behavior, she had never thought of that.

Adam looked piqued. He did not like being made a fool of.

"No more games, Finch." He warned. "Tell us everything. There's a cold blooded killer out there and it's my responsibility to apprehend him at the earliest."

"I was hired by a man in Chicago," Finch began. "You can have his details later. Well, my client didn't exactly lose his shirt, but he lost a considerable amount."

After he fell prey to one of Paddy's schemes, his client had to postpone his retirement and keep working at the ripe old age of seventy. The man had only one goal now. He wanted Paddy to pay for his sins.

"My brief was clear," Finch exclaimed. "Gather enough evidence against the man to put him away for the rest of his life."

It was not easy. Being an accomplished con man, Paddy had covered his tracks well. There was only one course open. Catch him in the act! The only way to get undeniable proof against the man.

Jenny was skeptical. What if Paddy had given up all that? He may have earned his fortune and planned to live the rest of his life on the straight and narrow. Was Finch going to be on his tail forever?

Adam echoed her thoughts and posed that question.

"A leopard cannot change his spots, Sheriff." Finch quipped. "I was positive he would slip soon. Luckily, Hank Smith gave him the right motivation."

The teacher may have thought he could hoodwink Paddy, but he was going to be outwitted. Paddy promised to get him funding in the form of government grants. He would have asked Smith to put up some money and absconded with it.

Jenny remembered how Paddy had urged her to franchise the Boardwalk Café. He had painted a rosy picture, picking up on what he thought was her greatest aspiration. Wasn't that how conmen operated? They got hold of your Achille's heel and applied the right amount of pressure until they got what they wanted.

Adam thought there was a flaw in Finch's story. Wasn't Paddy Australian? How could he claim to obtain grants from the US government?

"Oh that!" Finch threw back his head and laughed, managing to bewilder them. "Another lie, of course."

Jenny realized he was enjoying keeping them on tenterhooks.

"Paddy was as American as us." Finch dropped a bombshell.

His investigation had revealed the man's real name was Jimbo Sawyer.

"Born in a small Midwest town, raised in a trailer park. Absentee father, junkie mother. Jimbo went to Chicago and worked in a garage, doing odd jobs. Developed a liking for money, staring at all the rich people who brought their cars in." Finch sighed. "The garage had been a front for some shady business. One of them was a safe cracker who tried to teach him the trade. But Jimbo was better with words. He could easily talk people into parting with their money."

Long story short, Jimbo Sawyer had run some big cons, amassed a fortune and retired from the game. Nobody knew where he was until Finch tracked him to Pelican Cove.

"Let's not forget Hank Smith," Jenny stepped in. "Are you two working together?"

Finch shook his head. Adam wanted to know why Paddy or Jimbo had not recognized Smith.

"He never met Smith before. Many of the people he fleeced hadn't ever laid eyes on him."

Jenny's mind raced with alternate theories. Could they trust everything Finch was saying? He may be a private detective but what if he had taken matters in his own hands and gone one step ahead?

"You decided to please your client," Adam began. "So you got rid of Paddy. Took the ultimate revenge."

Johnny Finch turned sullen. He had said everything he was going to. If they had any more questions, they could talk to him through a lawyer.

"Why don't you check everything I have told you, Sheriff? My client will vouch for me. And for the record, I did not harm Paddy Benson or Shirley Brown."

They were at an impasse. Adam came out of the room, followed by Jenny.

"We have to let him go, at least for now."

Jenny thanked him for letting her sit in. She had to go back to the café.

"Lunch is on me today," she offered. "Any particular requests?"

Adam offered a lopsided smile. Whatever she cooked would be fine with him.

Jenny stepped out into a cold, dreary day. The ground was wet. There must have been a few showers while she was closeted in that windowless room. She took her time walking down the boardwalk, stifling a yawn.

The Magnolias were sipping coffee, engrossed in their own tasks. Betty Sue's hands moved in a furious rhythm, knitting a pink blanket. Molly's head was immersed in a book and Heather sported a broody look, playing with a salt shaker. Star must be in the kitchen. She came out just as Jenny went up the steps.

"You're back. I started some chicken soup, sweetie!"

Jenny thanked her and expressed her longing for some strong, hot coffee. Star pressed her to sit down. She came out with a fresh pot and a plate of muffins.

"So?" Heather cried after Jenny had added cream and sugar to her cup and taken a sip. "Did that man with the gun confess?"

Jenny broke a piece from a muffin and popped it in her mouth, shaking her head. Bit by bit, she narrated everything she had just heard, trying to answer all the questions the others threw at her.

"Jimbo what?" Betty Sue boomed. "He had the nerve to live here under a false name?"

Heather told her to calm down. Paddy had been a charming rogue who dazzled them with his smooth tongue. At least he had not swindled anyone in Pelican Cove.

"As far as we know," Molly corrected. "But the man's dead now and no longer a threat."

It was beginning to look like they would never find out what really happened.

"Now that we know his background, it's clear a lot of people must have wished him dead," Heather summed up. "It could have been unplanned. One of his victims came to Pelican Cove, recognized him, and got rid of him in a burst of anger."

That did not explain who murdered Shirley, Jenny reminded her.

"Finch may claim to be innocent, but I do not trust the man. He can't account for where he was on both occasions, which is a bit odd. There's always someone around, even if we are sparsely populated."

Heather argued there was no evidence. She asked Jenny to remember the house where Paddy had been found. There were no prints in the house.

Jenny sat up with a jerk, spilling coffee on her dress.

"What did you say?"

With a dramatic roll of her eyes, Heather deigned to repeat herself.

"There are no prints anywhere in the house. No way to prove Johnny Finch was there."

Jenny beamed. A lightbulb had just gone on in her head. The truth had been staring them in the face all along.

"You up for a drive?" she asked Heather. "Chop – chop!"

Chapter 26

The sky cleared as the shadows lengthened. A fierce wind blew most of the dark storm clouds away, providing a clear view of the setting sun. Jenny gazed at the golden orb as it skimmed the horizon, unable to believe how things had developed.

"You shouldn't have gone there alone." Adam was stern.

"I was with her," Heather piped up. "Why don't you relax, Adam? You have your man."

Jenny added that they had managed to avert any mishap.

Shaking his head as he muttered under his breath, Adam screeched to a stop outside Seaview. Jason paced the porch. Star sat in a wicker chair, looking worried.

"We're in for a lecture," Jenny sighed. "I do love them so! How'd I get so lucky?"

Jason had wrapped her in his arms the moment she stepped out of his car.

"It's about time!"

He glared at Adam.

"You have a lot to answer for."

Star had tears in her eyes.

"Where have you been, Jenny? You've been gone for hours! We had no update, no idea what was happening."

Their voices brought Betty Sue and Billy outside.

"I didn't expect this kind of tomfoolery from you, Jenny. Did Heather talk you into it?"

Jenny couldn't stop smiling. Heather didn't have any snarky comeback. They all trooped in and headed to the living room. The house was filled with the savory smells of tomato and oregano.

"Do I smell lasagna?" Jenny squealed. "I'm starving!"

Star nodded. Her six cheese lasagna was baking in the oven. It would be ready in thirty minutes.

"I'll put out some munchies until then."

Jason had already decanted a couple of bottles of wine. He poured it and handed out the glasses. Star provided a generous spread, with pimento cheese, crab dip, crackers and some dried fruit and nuts.

Everyone held back on their questions until the newcomers had a few bites. Jenny knew they were being kind.

"We caught the man," Adam began. "He confessed to the murder of Paddy alias Jimbo and Shirley Brown."

Jason wanted to know if his wife had played a role. Adam didn't hesitate to give her credit. Her quick thinking had allowed them to apprehend the man in time.

"Start at the beginning," Betty Sue interrupted. "What happened when you took off like a bullet from the café this morning?"

Jenny felt all the eyes in the room swing toward her.

"Heather and I drove to the motel."

Star wanted to know what they hoped to find there.

"Rio Harris." Jenny replied. "The man who was renting the house where Paddy was found."

What did she want with him, Billy asked.

Jenny brought up what they had been talking about that morning. The police had found no fingerprints at the location of Paddy's murder. The only fingerprints on the knife belonged to Shirley. This did not make sense because a man had supposedly been living there until the previous evening. That meant one thing. The place had been wiped clean.

"Why would he kill Paddy though?" Star wanted to know. "Did they know each other?"

Jenny told them her theory.

"This is what I thought after we learned the truth about Paddy Benson. He was trying to swindle Hank Smith, right? Maybe he was trying the same thing with other people? Rio Harris must be another of his victims. But he realized what

Paddy was up to. They had an argument and Harris plunged a knife in him in the heat of the moment."

What did she hope to achieve by talking to the man, Jason quizzed. His brows were drawn together and his mouth was set in a firm line.

Jenny immediately felt guilty for worrying him. She had not realized the danger she was in until much later.

"I'm sorry, Jase! Heather and I came up with a plan. We offered to have a scoop for him and invited him to the café. Then we swiped his cup."

They had rushed to the police station and asked him to run the man's fingerprints.

"And you went along with it?" Jason stared at Adam.

"What can I say, they were both very persuasive."

Betty Sue gave a grunt, making her opinion clear. Adam had been taken in.

The prints revealed something they could never have guessed. Rio Harris was a crook. He had an arrest record a mile long and had been in and out of prison.

"Armed robbery," Adam informed them. "That meant he was prone to violence. He had been accused of murder once but nothing was proven."

The police had wasted no time in rushing to the motel. Harris was brought in for questioning. Adam hinted they might have found his finger prints on the murder weapon. The man lost his composure and blurted out that he had taken care to wipe them before leaving the scene of the crime.

But he refused to say any more.

Billy's phone rang, startling them. It was Nick. He wanted to know if Jenny was safe. She took the phone from him and walked to the kitchen and spent the next few minutes reassuring him. When she hung up, she realized her hand was shaking. Talking to her son had brought home how much she valued her life and the people in it.

Star came into the kitchen just as the oven dinged. She pulled on some mitts and pulled out a couple of pans of steaming lasagna.

"It has to rest for a while."

She set the pans on the counter and began tossing the salad.

"Are you okay, sweetie?"

Jenny pulled herself together and nodded. She had been more circumspect than usual and they had a positive outcome.

"I'm fine. Just hungry for that lasagna."

Heather was setting the table in the dining room. Everyone was already seated. They had been waiting for her.

"Kids!" she gave a mock sigh. "Nick's like an old woman."

Adam took up the narrative.

"Harris summoned me after I let him stew for a while. He wanted a lawyer. Jenny came in and told him she understood his plight. Paddy had fooled him."

The man's ego was his downfall. He told them he was too sharp to be taken in by a confidence trickster.

"Then why did he murder him?" Billy frowned. "The man must have a motive."

Adam and Jenny both nodded. Paddy had been blackmailing Rio Harris.

"We learnt Harris was a safe cracker, right? He and his cronies met in Pelican Cove to plan a big heist. They figured it was the best place for such a tryst – remote island, deserted in winter etc. But Paddy overheard them."

He had threatened Harris with exposure and demanded a big sum.

"The money wasn't a problem according to Harris." Adam gave a dry laugh. "He didn't want any loose ends."

"He recognized Paddy for the crook he was," Heather smirked. "Decided he could not trust him."

So Rio Harris had made an elaborate plan. He rented the house and stayed there for a few days, watching Paddy's movements. He had appeased Paddy by making small payments, promising him a big payoff on a certain day.

"There was nothing wrong with the heater, of course," Jenny told them. "Harris rigged it and booked a room in the motel. He called his landlord and lodged a complaint, knowing it would be afternoon by the time the man arrived from the city."

Harris set up an appointment to meet Paddy in the rented house that morning. Expecting his bag of gold, Paddy never suspected a thing. Harris attacked him and finished him off. He had already wiped all the surfaces the previous night to make sure there were no finger prints that could be traced back to him. Then he wore gloves while committing the murder.

"We'll never know how Shirley's print ended up on that knife," Adam sighed.

Jenny agreed they could only speculate. Clearly, she had gone to the house with Paddy. But she left before Harris arrived.

"She had this habit of eating something every hour or so. Said her blood sugar dropped if she didn't nibble on something. She must have used the knife to cut a fruit or something."

Adam's eyes gleamed.

"Jenny! You might have hit upon the right explanation. We found half an apple on the kitchen counter. I've been puzzling over it for some time."

That is how Shirley's finger print ended up on the knife.

Star asked Heather to dish out the salad. Then she cut big slices of the lasagna and served them.

"Why did this man kill Shirley though?" she asked.

Adam and Jenny's visit to the motel spooked him.

"Harris had no idea if Paddy had shared any details of the upcoming heist with her. But he was not taking any chances."

Shirley's image flashed before Jenny's eyes, her stylish persona and her pricey shoes. She had possessed a certain poise. But the poor woman had been an innocent victim.

"Was Harris the one who placed that threatening note on your windshield?" Jason asked.

Jenny nodded. He thought it would scare her.

"Little did he know ..." Adam quipped.

Chapter 27

Jenny had slaved in the kitchen for the past two days, testing her flan recipe. She narrowed it down to three different flavors. One was closest to the classic caramel flan, except she had opted for a salted version. The second was a dark chocolate flan drenched in spiced raspberry sauce. A sweet and tart mango flan completed the trio.

She had used tiny ramekins and baked a dozen of each. The day of reckoning was here. All her friends were invited to taste the flans and rate them. The winner would be added to the new menu at the Boardwalk Café.

Nick sauntered into the kitchen and placed an arm around Jenny's shoulders.

"They look great, Mom. In fact, can you let me have one right now?"

She wagged her finger at him, shaking her head.

"Wait until the others get here."

They had set up a taco bar. Billy and Jason were outside, starting up the grill. Captain Charlie supervised their efforts, giving directions.

Betty Sue, Heather and Molly were on their way. Jenny had high hopes for what the day would bring.

"Did you have the talk?" Nick inquired. "Are you going to share what went down between the two of you?"

Jenny decided to give him a quick overview.

She had coaxed Heather into going for a drive with her, on the pretext of checking out some wicker furniture for the café. The intention was to have a heart to heart talk with no interruptions. She had hoped Heather would be more open if she thought the others were not around to dissect what she said. It had been just what she needed.

Her thoughts traveled back to the day. She had openly confronted Heather.

"Am I the reason you fell out with Billy?"

Always a straight shooter, Heather turned red but hesitated before giving a nod.

"How could you think he's in love with me?" Jenny burst out. "Think of everything Billy's done for you over the past year. He actually bought a house in Pelican Cove, just to be close to you. That's a man who's spent most of his life where the action is. He only has eyes for you, Heather."

Heather finally voiced her concerns. Billy got nostalgic when he talked about his past life with Jenny. When he had driven by their old house in northern Virginia, his eyes had been full of longing. Then he had taken them to the restaurant Jenny liked and waxed on about how it had been their favorite for twenty years.

"You have so much history with him," she cried. "I'm just the flavor of the month."

Jenny had been aghast.

"Are you jealous? Don't be." She had struggled to choose her words. "I can't erase the past and I won't apologize for it. Our past will be a part of our life, especially since we have a son. He will refer to it even if we don't."

Heather had wilted before her eyes. But Jenny wasn't done.

"You have known all this from day one. Billy was always honest with you, wasn't he?" Jenny paused. "Do you think we'll get back together?"

Heather's eyes widened.

"No. I can see how much you love Jason."

They sat there, in a small café off the Interstate, sipping coffee, neither sure what to say next. Jenny felt a burst of anger in her chest.

"Ultimately, Heather. It's a leap of faith. But I don't approve of the way you treated Billy. Very shabby and thoughtless." She hissed. "Betty Sue's right. You will never settle down. You have a heart of stone!"

Nick shook her arm, startling her.

"Is that all? What's the outcome, Mom?"

The doorbell chimed before Jenny could answer him. The subject of their discussion sauntered in, wearing a breezy dress Jenny had never seen before. It softened her looks and made Heather look much younger. Were those highlights in her hair?

"You look nice," she complimented. "But it's fifty degrees outside. You're going to freeze to death."

"That's what I told her," Betty Sue grumbled.

The bell rang again and Star arrived with Jimmy Parsons. She had spent the day at the Boardwalk Café, working on her mural.

"How long will the café be closed?" Molly asked. "I guess we won't be meeting for coffee until then."

Jenny told them the kitchen would be closed for a week or two. She would be doing a limited number of deliveries for her customers during that time, cooking in her home kitchen at Seaview. But the deck would be free for their use most of the time and they could still meet there every morning.

"I have two large thermoses that I can get the coffee in. There's no way I'm giving up coffee hour."

They all agreed it was necessary for survival.

Betty Sue offered the use of the Bayview Inn. Molly could easily walk there from the library. So could Star who would be at the café for most of the day, painting the murals.

Captain Charlie came in through the back door and began to herd them out.

"The grill's hot and the meat will be ready in a trice. Grab your plates, ladies."

Clear skies greeted them, festooned in various shades of pink and mauve. The sun was a bright orange ball, suspended in the sky. The breeze carried the scent of the sea, mingled with the blooms from Jenny's garden.

Trestle tables dressed in colorful cloths groaned with bowls of salsa, guacamole, beans and cheese. Molly had brought a couple of salads. Billy mixed margaritas for everyone while Jason took the meat off the grill and loaded it on a platter.

"Save room for dessert." Jenny reminded them. "Don't forget you're here to taste the flan."

None of them could resist the tacos. Nick declared a prize for the most delicious combination and that set everyone off.

Betty Sue won. Her version of grilled steak, charred pineapple, ancho salsa with pepperjack cheese and jalapenos was declared the most original.

"What do I get, young man?" she thundered, a rare twinkle in her eyes.

"How 'bout a picnic on the beach?" Nick bantered. "Just the two of us. Or a dinner date wherever you want."

Betty Sue beamed and asked him to set it up.

They sat in a circle around the fire pit, sated, enjoying the golden twilight. Heather suggested a walk.

"You kids go ahead," Betty Sue replied. "I'm going to warm myself by the fire."

"We can go later, Grandma. I think we're all too full to move."

Jason brought up the winter festival.

"So you had the last word as usual, eh, Betty Sue?" he chuckled. "We can all enjoy some peace until spring."

His words didn't go down well. Jenny was surprised to see Betty Sue's eyes darken, her mouth settling in a pout.

"You're wrong, Jason. Nobody gives a whit about our traditions and the laws the town committee has set up. Haven't you heard about that silly survey?"

Jenny had been so engrossed in talking to the contractors, finalizing the work to be done on the cafe, she had not had time to pick up any of the latest gossip.

"What do you mean, Betty Sue?"

Someone, probably one of the new residents, had placed stacks of a questionnaire at certain places in town. The grocery store owned by the Williams family was one such spot. There was a box in which people could put in their filled out forms.

"Every form gets them a five dollar coupon at the store," Heather supplied. "Chris told me people are lining up outside and the store is doing a roaring business."

Molly admitted the same thing was happening at the library, although they could not offer any monetary incentive.

"And what kind of survey is this?" Jenny was curious.

It centered around food. What kind of restaurants people wanted to see in Pelican Cove, the type of cuisine they liked and how much they were willing to spend on it. There were questions about ambience and travel time.

"How is that relevant?" Molly wondered out loud. "It doesn't take more than ten minutes to cross the town."

Star asked why this had not been discussed at the town meeting.

"They never sought our permission!" Betty Sue fumed. "According to the rules, the town committee must approve any communication which is addressed to the citizens at large. No, no. Whoever is behind this is purposely flaunting them."

Jenny pointed out what they were missing.

"This must be related to that new restaurant everyone was talking about. But why so hush hush?"

Captain Charlie confessed he had something to share. He sported a sheepish look, making everyone sit up and pay attention.

"I have been approached for a little job. Three hours every evening. The money's good."

"To do what?" Betty Sue exclaimed.

The old salt gave a shrug. He assumed they wanted him to run a boat.

They agreed it sounded mysterious. Betty Sue thought it was all very shady and was a portent of things to come.

Heather stood up and stretched. She was ready for her walk.

"Enough of this morbid talk. Let's work up an appetite for Jenny's flan."

Star convinced Betty Sue to join everyone. Jenny felt a bubble of excitement rise within her. She glanced at Nick, asking him a silent question. He gave a small shrug.

The beach was deserted. They walked in a wide line at first, then split into groups. Heather wove her arm into Billy's and pulled him ahead of the rest. They walked on for a few paces, beginning to shiver in the cold.

"Shall we head back?" Jason turned to Jenny.

"Shhhh ..." she clutched his hand and halted. "Do you see that?"

Heather and Billy faced each other, holding hands. She got down on one knee.

"Let's move closer," Jenny hissed. "I want to hear this."

Star and Betty Sue had caught up with them by then.

"You can begin," Nick called out, and was immediately hushed by the women around him.

Tears flew down Heather's face and she struggled to speak.

"I have been a fool, Billy. Will you forgive me for giving you such a hard time?"

He barely managed a nod. Jenny marveled how a man who chattered nineteen to the dozen most of the time could be tongue tied.

"You already know most of my faults," Heather continued. "So I won't bother listing them now. I thought I was incapable of love. Then you came into my life. You made everything fun. You let me be myself." Her breath hitched. "You never tried to change me, Billy. I didn't notice when I began to fall in love."

"You love me?" He gently urged her to stand up. "But I have a past, my dear sweet darling. And I am so much older than you."

She had been selfish but she was coming around.

"I guess Grandma spoiled me after all. I never had to share her with anyone."

Heather told him she had realized her mistake. All she asked for was a piece of his heart. He had plenty of love to share. And a family was not made of just two people.

Jenny heard Betty Sue sniffle. She moved close to her, hugging her from one side. She held her other arm out to Molly.

They stood like that, huddled together, watching the pair before them with bated breath.

"Billy, I love you and cannot imagine life without you. But I understand if your feelings have changed."

The ladies moved a few steps closer. Jenny saw Heather's chest heave as she took a deep breath.

"Will you marry me?"

Billy swooped her up in his arms and whooped with delight. The Magnolias began clapping. Jason and Captain Charlie whistled. Everyone began hugging each other.

"Wait a minute, wait a minute!" Nick bellowed. "You have to answer her, Dad."

Billy took Heather's face in his hands and stared into her eyes.

"Yes, I will."

**

Enjoying solving mysteries in Pelican Cove? Stay tuned for more in the next book in the series.

Chapter 28

Thank you for loving the Pelican Cove series. Your continued appreciation and interest keeps me motivated to write the next book. I am so grateful you gave this book a chance.

I would also like to thank my beta readers for pointing out those hard to spot errors that creep in despite several rounds of editing.

Thank you to everyone who writes to me or chimes in on social and spreads the word about my books. I really appreciate it.

Many thanks to my wonderful family who lend a hand in various ways to ensure this book comes to you. They are the rock I lean on, be it summer or winter.

Books by Leena Clover
Pelican Cove Cozy Mystery Series

Strawberries and Strangers – Pelican Cove Cozy Mystery Book 1

https://www.amazon.com/dp/B07CSW34GB/

Cupcakes and Celebrities – Pelican Cove Cozy Mystery Book 2

https://www.amazon.com/dp/B07CYX5TNR

Berries and Birthdays – Pelican Cove Cozy Mystery Book 3

https://www.amazon.com/gp/product/B07D7GG8KV

Sprinkles and Skeletons – Pelican Cove Cozy Mystery Book 4

https://www.amazon.com/dp/B07DW91NKG

Waffles and Weekends – Pelican Cove Cozy Mystery Book 5

https://www.amazon.com/dp/B07FRJ1FC1/

Muffins and Mobsters – Pelican Cove Cozy Mystery Book 6

LEENA CLOVER

https://www.amazon.com/dp/B07GRBCZG8/
Parfaits and Paramours – Pelican Cove Cozy Mystery Book 7
https://www.amazon.com/dp/B07K5G2DDJ
Truffles and Troubadours – Pelican Cove Cozy Mystery 8
https://www.amazon.com/dp/B07N6FQTK2/
Sundaes and Sinners– Pelican Cove Cozy Mystery 9
https://www.amazon.com/dp/B07PXYPNG5/
Croissants and Cruises– Pelican Cove Cozy Mystery 10
https://www.amazon.com/dp/B082L2W6V2
Pancakes and Parrots– Pelican Cove Cozy Mystery 11
https://www.amazon.com/dp/B082H1DJ42
Cookies and Christmas – Pelican Cove Cozy Mystery 12
https://www.amazon.com/dp/ B08FB1TTCJ
Popsicles and Poisons
Biscuits and Butlers
https://www.amazon.com/dp/B09HGZ9FTH

Dolphin Bay Cozy Mystery Series
Raspberry Chocolate Murder – Dolphin Bay Cozy Mystery Book 1
https://www.amazon.com/dp/B07VVQDGPN
Orange Thyme Death – Dolphin Bay Cozy Mystery Book 2
https://www.amazon.com/dp/B07W226H71
Apple Caramel Mayhem – Dolphin Bay Cozy Mystery Book 3

https://www.amazon.com/dp/B07YN35K2Y

Cranberry Sage Miracle – Dolphin Bay Cozy Mystery Book 4

https://www.amazon.com/dp/B08538MP3Z

Blueberry Chai Frenzy- Dolphin Bay Cozy Mystery Book 5

https://www.amazon.com/dp/B08CTC9M5G

Mango Chili Cruiser

https://www.amazon.com/dp/B08XY1D5Q2

Strawberry Vanilla Peril

https://www.amazon.com/dp/B08XY368ZP

Cherry Lime Havoc

https://www.amazon.com/dp/B098P6M1S7

Pumpkin Ginger Bedlam

https://www.amazon.com/dp/B09JYHGS8P

Meera Patel Cozy Mystery Series

Gone with the Wings – Meera Patel Cozy Mystery Book 1

https://www.amazon.com/dp/B071WHNM6K

A Pocket Full of Pie - Meera Patel Cozy Mystery Book 2

https://www.amazon.com/dp/B072Q7B47P/

For a Few Dumplings More - Meera Patel Cozy Mystery Book 3

https://www.amazon.com/dp/B072V3T2BV

Back to the Fajitas - Meera Patel Cozy Mystery Book 4

https://www.amazon.com/dp/B0748KPTLM

Christmas with the Franks – Meera Patel Cozy Mystery Book 5

https://www.amazon.com/gp/product/B077GXR4WS/

British Cozy Mystery Series

Murder at Buxley Manor

https://www.amazon.com/dp/B0BVG7V2DY

Murder at Castle Morse

https://www.amazon.com/gp/product/B0BX8XB27G

Murder at Ridley Hall

https://www.amazon.com/dp/B0CBQCSFZF

Meg Butler Cruise Cozy Series

Sail Away Patsy

https://www.amazon.com/dp/B09XHY3PBG

Bingo Bashed

https://www.amazon.com/dp/B0BZKK6FWX

Suite Knife

Casino Foil

https://www.amazon.com/dp/B0D187JVZ3

Printed in Dunstable, United Kingdom